A Child Called Happiness

STEPHAN COLLISHAW

Legend Press Ltd, 107-111 Fleet Street, London, EC4A 2AB
info@legend-paperbooks.co.uk | www.legendpress.co.uk

 British Library Cataloguing in Publication Data available.

Print ISBN 978-1-7871988-1-4
Ebook ISBN 978-1-7871988-0-7
Set in Times. Printing managed by Jellyfish Solutions Ltd
Cover design by Gudrun Jobst | www.yotedesign.com

Stephan Collishaw was brought up on a council estate and failed all of his O-levels. His first novel *The Last Girl* (2003) was chosen by the *Independent on Sunday* as one of its Novels of the Year. In 2004 Stephan was selected as one of the British Council's 20 best young British novelists. His first novel with Legend Press, *The Song of the Stork*, was published in 2017 and described by William Ryan as 'An elegantly crafted, beautifully written novel about love, survival and hope against all the odds.'

Stephan now works as a teacher in Nottingham, having also lived and worked abroad in Lithuania and Mallorca, where his son Lukas was born.

Follow Stephan on Twitter
@scollishaw

‘Freedom is not something that one people can bestow on another as a gift. They claim it as their own and none can keep it from them.’

Kwame Nkrumah

Mazowe Valley
Zimbabwe
2011

1

They had almost reached the gates of the farm when Natalie heard the sharp wail. At first she thought it was the cry of a bird, but as she listened it subsided into a gurgling sob, soft and all too human. She glanced around but could see nothing. At the foot of the slope, her uncle turned his horse and waved impatiently. Natalie held up her hand. She was about to move forward when she heard it again, to her left.

Turning in her saddle, she scanned the undergrowth and the low brush. She nudged the horse closer to the thicket and the granite boulders, peering into the shadows. The irritation was clear in her uncle's posture as he turned his horse and began to make his way back up the slope.

'What is it?'

'I heard a cry.'

Natalie slipped down off the horse.

'It was probably a bird.'

'No,' she said. 'It wasn't a bird.'

'What kind of a cry?'

Natalie didn't have to answer as the thin wail rose again, insistent and clear above the noise of the cicadas and rock thrush.

'Up there.'

They had set out early from the farm, before the sun had

risen and it had just begun to get light as they started the climb up the long, slow hill back home again. All around, Natalie could hear the sound of the morning: the squeak of the boulder chaff, the reeling martins. They had ascended from woodland and ahead, at the crest of the kopje, three large boulders were balanced one on top of the other, as if placed there by some giant. They pulled their horses up side-by-side and gazed at them in silence.

'Drew's Kopje,' Roy, her uncle said, motioning with his hand. 'Named after your great-uncle.'

Natalie nodded. She was about to move the horse forward, but her uncle held out his hand and stopped her. The early morning air was cold and slightly damp from the night. It had been colder than Natalie had anticipated. The breath of the horses lingered in the air.

'Wait,' her uncle said.

The horses were content to stand there, lowering their heads to feed on the coarse tufty grass. Natalie cast a quick sidelong glance at Roy, a stern man in his late fifties. His hair was short and greying; his face tanned deeply, like leather. There was not a spare inch of flesh on him. He was a man of few words and Natalie felt uncomfortable in his presence. Looking at him now, in the early morning light, she could see almost no resemblance to her mother, a soft-featured, gentle, bookish woman.

'See?'

The light was changing, almost as if the brush around them had begun to glow from some internal energy. A moment later the top boulder flamed, brilliantly illuminated. Within minutes, the three rocks were consumed, glistening in the light of the rising sun.

'Incredible,' Natalie breathed.

Her uncle nodded, nudging his horse forward along a narrow path that cut up the side of the hill around the glowing stones.

'The natives used to consider this a sacred place. Home to

their ancestral spirits.'

The farm at the bottom of the hill, which they were circling back towards, was at the end of the Mazowe Valley in northern Zimbabwe. It was fertile land, though its careful cultivation had begun to look a little dilapidated. As they drove in on the road from Harare, Natalie had noted the number of farms that had fallen into disrepair; agricultural machinery rusted gently, unused, in the blistering sun. Here and there, on these farms, elderly men worked small patches of the red soil with primitive implements, pausing, briefly from their labour to watch as the wheels of the Land Rover sang past on the hot tarmac.

There were other farms, though, large, neatly trimmed estates; evidence that commercial farming was continuing. Large citrus orchards stretched away into the distance and up near Bindura a copper mine scarred the beauty. The Drew farm was at the far end of the valley. Steep hills rose around it, granite capped, frilled with lush, dark vegetation. The main farmhouse was large and airy, with oak panelled walls, and a large veranda from which you could look out not only across the farm, but along the road to Bindura, and the surrounding countryside.

As they rode up over the back of Drew's Kopje, Natalie saw the large Jacaranda that marked the gateway to the farm. In the early morning sunlight, its blue flowers glowed hazily. It was hard to gaze out across the landscape and not be moved by the large cerulean expanse of sky, the granite kopjes, the purple hills in the distance, the thin line of smoke rising from the thatched roofed village huts, the elegant Jacaranda carpeting the dirt with its blossom. Natalie hesitated a moment, letting her uncle draw ahead. She stopped the horse on the crown of the hill and breathed in deeply.

The air was alive with the sound of insects and birds. Yet at the same time it seemed silent. There was not, she realised, the sound of a single engine. No car. No plane. She listened intently. Nothing but the sounds of nature. Natalie wasn't sure she had ever experienced this pure absence of noise before. Even the previous night, as she sat on the veranda of her cottage and listened to the bellow of bullfrogs, there had been the sound of the generator, and somewhere in the main house the low, muffled, melancholy of American country music on the radio.

There was something primordial about this peacefulness. Something deeply moving. She exhaled slowly, breathing out all the pain and the darkness.

It was then, as she rode down towards the farm, trailing her uncle, that she heard the sound of crying.

'Where did it come from?' her uncle asked, pulling his horse round and riding back up to Natalie.

'Up there.'

Natalie pushed through the branches, the thorns scratching at the red uncovered skin on her forearms and scrambled up onto the boulders. The baby lay on the top, nestled within the smooth indentation on its surface, swaddled loosely in a dirty rag. It could have been no more than a few weeks old. She dropped down onto her knees beside the little bundle, her heart thumping. She half reached out to touch the exposed plump cheek, but stopped herself. The baby looked up at her, its eyes a dark brown, tinged with blue. Her fingers fluttered across her belly.

'Anything up there?'

'Yes,' she called back down to her uncle. She paused, breathless.

The baby was silent, fascinated by her; the small eyes following her every move. As it breathed out, small bubbles burst on its lips. Dribble trickled down its cheek, settling in the shell of its ear. Mucus frothed freshly from its wide nostrils. The small, dark forehead was smooth, though the skin flaked a little, and beneath its eyes stark creases gave it a look of world-weary knowingness. She listened to the sound of its breaths, shallow, light as the whispers of wind in the dry grass. Her uncle's head appeared close behind her.

'What is it?'

'A child,' Natalie said. 'A baby.'

'Pass it down.'

She had never held a child before. She wasn't sure how to pick it up. Gently pushing her fingers under the body, she levered it into her hands. The baby watched her. It felt so light, almost no weight at all. She cradled it in the crook of her arm and touched its cheek with her right hand; the baby gazed up at her, deep into her eyes with the wisdom of ages and she felt her heart turn. A bubble rose from the core of her being and a pressure built behind her eyes. Her throat constricted and her eyes began to glaze. Suddenly she felt tears streaming down her cheeks and the bubble tight and hard in her throat.

'Pass it to me,' her uncle said.

His voice was gentle and though he must have seen the tears he did not mention them. Natalie passed the baby across the hot stone to her uncle, who took it naturally and, holding it high, turned and worked his way back through the bush towards the waiting horses.

'Do you think the mother is around somewhere?' Natalie asked.

She had brushed the tears from her face with the cuff of her shirt, but still she avoided meeting her uncle's eyes.

'Can you see anyone?' her uncle answered matter-of-factly.

'No.'

'Anyone there?' her uncle called, his voice echoing from the boulders and down the cleft they had arisen from, bouncing from one kopje to another. The insects sang. Birds flittered away, startled, from the tops of the trees, and something scurried in the undergrowth a few feet away.

'If it had been left there the birds would have had it before the morning was out,' Roy said. 'That or an animal. It wouldn't last long.'

'Who do you think left it there?'

'It looks fairly new-born.'

'But why?'

Her uncle shrugged. 'Perhaps they couldn't afford to raise it.'

'And just left it to die?'

When she had mounted her horse, she took the baby from Roy, holding it tight. The baby began to cry and she loosened it a little, holding it nervously. She tried speaking to it, but she didn't know what to say.

'You'll be okay with it?' her uncle asked.

She nodded, taking the track slowly. As they passed beneath the Jacaranda it showered them with blue flowers so that when they arrived on the farm, they were confettied with delicate petals, Natalie with the baby lulled to sleep.

Her aunt Kristine's face, when she saw them, was a mixture of laughter and concern.

2

Kare kare. Long, long ago. I can still remember the day my father died; I was four years old. But this story does not start then. No. We shall get to his story by and by. This story begins in the days of my grandfather, in the days of the first Chimurenga – the first uprising.

These fields were ours then; these hills, this earth. Our village nestled in between the boulders on the side of the valley. There were many huts. The large central hut belonged to my grandfather. His cattle roamed the whole region from the ridge to the other side of the valley. He had three wives, of which my grandmother was the youngest. He was already an old man when he took her as wife. It was a fertile land, rich and fruitful. The village was close to that of the spirit guide, Nehanda, and like many, he revered her.

His name was Tafara. *We are happy*, it means, in the Shona language.

It was the year 1896, though Tafara would not have known it as that.

Tafara had settled himself at the top of a high ridge as darkness fell across the valley. In his hands he held the stick that had belonged to his father. It had been a year since his death and the next day they would be visiting his grave to perform the ceremony. Back in the village the women were brewing beer and preparing the *sadza*; it was just possible to hear the sound of voices and music drifting up over the dry grassland.

Tafara lay back against the stone, which was warm still from the sun. The night was heavy, the darkness, like a hot stifling blanket, blocked out any gleam of light. The moon had not yet risen, but as he lay there the stars began to appear, a glittering sweep of lights, pinpricks of brilliance. Billowing clouds were massed along the horizon, apparent only from the thick black absence of starlight. The rains had held off. Normally they would have come by now. Dark clouds gathered and drifted restlessly across the sky, but no rain had fallen. It had been a poor season; ever since his father had died, the earth seemed to have shrivelled up. The ground was bone hard.

Tafara hugged the stick to his chest and tried to picture his father's face, but found he could not. He closed his eyes and delineated the details, the beard, the prominent forehead, the noble bearing; but the parts would not stitch together. His voice, though, remained and Tafara could hear it now, laying there, as if it had been only minutes before that it had breathed in his ear.

'*Sango rinopa waneta*.'

The forest rewards you when you are weary.

They had been his father's last words, his voice soft and flutelike as he lay upon his deathbed. Tafara felt now the soft weight of his father's hand on his head. Heard the exhaustion in his voice. Saw still, piercingly clearly, the slow rise and fall of his emaciated chest beneath the thin blanket.

'Yes, father,' he had whispered.

But he did not know what his father had meant. Was it a criticism? Was it encouragement? This was Tafara's sixteenth season of rains and he felt ill-prepared for the responsibilities about to fall upon him as the eldest son.

A sudden noise disturbed his thoughts. Alert, he sat up, his ears straining. The darkness was impenetrable; it was barely possible for him to see his hand in front of his face. Slowly and silently he slipped the long knife from his belt. His hand was trembling, but he breathed deeply, slowed the race of his heart and raised himself onto the balls of his bare feet. Somewhere a little below him he could hear movement in the undergrowth. A low rustle. He listened intently trying to gauge the size of the creature making the noise, listening for its breathing, for the sounds that might identify it, but little carried.

He eased himself down from the rock, placing its smooth surface against his back, taking care to detect the direction of the soft breeze. He flared his nostrils, inhaled deeply, analysing the scents in the air. Wood smoke. He dropped to a squat. The village was behind him on the other side of the ridge and the breeze was blowing away from it. It was thin, a small fire. He eased forwards silently. As he crept over the ridge he saw the soft glow of the flames, half way down the incline.

He moved to within thirty feet of the fire, keeping low. His view was partly obscured by high brush and he had to work around them, dipping below some large boulders and through a small copse of Msasa. He had crept closer than he anticipated. Two men were seated by the small fire. The first was of middling height dressed in a khaki green jacket. His hat had been discarded next to him. The second sat on the opposite side of the fire and little was visible of him beyond his gaunt face and beard.

It was not the first time Tafara had seen white men; they had been making incursions through the region more and more regularly. A small group of men had visited his father more than a year before, wanting to purchase land at the head of the valley where they had found deposits of gold. His father had turned them away. One of the white men had taken a large box from the back of their cart and erected it in front of the village. He had assembled the villagers in front of one of the huts and then disappeared beneath a black sheet in front of them. Tafara recalled the incident now and smiled, remembering their incomprehension at the behaviour of this white man hidden beneath his sheet before them.

Sometime later he came out from under it, grinned at them and laughed, and they laughed too at his madness. But, before he left, the white man presented them with a little miracle. On a card, no larger than the width and length of his hand, he presented them with the image of themselves as they had been at that moment, stood before the hut. Tafara did not understand what he had done, but he cherished that small miracle the white man gave him and kept it safely among his possessions.

For a while he watched the two men passing a small canteen between themselves, talking in low voices. When he was assured that they posed no danger he crept away, circling the kopje, moving silently, his ears alert for more of the white men; but the night was quiet.

The village glowed in the deep night and voices and music were audible as soon as he crossed the ridge. A cow had been slaughtered earlier in the day and the rich smell of the meat hung heavily in the air, making his mouth water as he made his way back. There was singing and the sound of the *mbira*. Many of the men were drunk when he passed through the village towards the central hut. Kamba, his uncle, was sprawled out in the shadows snoring loudly.

Tafara slept fitfully and was woken by a deep grumble shortly before dawn. For some moments he lay listening, but the village was silent and he drifted back to sleep.

They woke very early the following day, and taking the *sadza* that had been prepared and the beer, they made their way to the burial site of Chimukoko. The weather was heavy and uncomfortable, the air tense as though it might snap. Spreading out the food upon the grave, the women gathered around, a low chant rising rhythmically in the gathering dawn light. They poured the libations of beer across the ground.

At the appointed time, Tafara was motioned forward. He stood nervously and glanced across at his uncle. Kamba was the younger brother of his father and many of the tribe looked to him for authority. Kamba's head was lowered and his hand rested on his large belly. He had dragged his feet all the way to the burial ground, hung over from the previous evening's excesses. Raising his head slightly, he glanced at Tafara and nodded slowly, barely perceptibly, before letting his chin settle back against the rolls of fat on his chest.

'*Mudzimu*!' Tafara called out, kneeling before the grave. 'Spirits hear! We welcome you back home. Come guide your family. If there is anything you need, please let us know. Have patience with us. Treat us with mercy.'

The earth shook. The heavens clapped with rage and the burial ground was illuminated by a brilliant, jagged flash of light. A sudden silence descended upon the mourners, and Tafara felt his heart rise into his mouth. He jumped to his feet.

'*Mudzimu*!' he called.

Following the brilliant light, the day seemed plunged into darkness. The clouds had been gathering since dawn and hung heavily now over the tops of the baobabs and Msasa. As he lifted his face to the sky he felt the first drop of water. He grinned. And suddenly it was raining; hard, large pellets of water that slapped against the skin and sizzled against the hot earth and rock. A torrential outpouring, which, as they made their way back to the village obscured their view, ran down their bodies, formed a liquid curtain across their path. The red earth stained their feet and ankles, and rode up their legs; it squelched between their toes as they walked.

The huts were warm and dry. Tafara sat in the centre of the largest, the sound of the *mbira* and drums drowning out the rain. His head swam with the beer and his senses were stimulated by the scent of the roasted calf and the *duiker*. He felt taller, more assured; he noted the respect in the voices of the women who brought him food.

Across the fire sat Kamba, his lips glossy with the juices of the meat they had eaten. Kamba smiled. His face jumped in the heat that rose from the fire.

'You have your father's blessing,' Kamba said.

Tafara nodded. 'Sometimes I am frightened,' he said.

Kamba waved his hand dismissively. 'There is no reason to be afraid. Your father's spirit will guide you. You are a young, strong man. For generations our family has lived on these lands and your children's children will remember you in these same caves. What greater blessing could you want?'

'My father was a wise man.'

'And in time so shall you be. Listen to the spirits. Listen to the elders. Love the land. That is all that is asked of you.'

That night, Tafara returned to his young bride. It was dark when he went in to her and she was sleeping already. When he lay down beside her, she stirred and awoke, her eyes opening, blinking in the darkness, the faint light of the moon falling through the open door reflecting weakly in her large eyes. She murmured something, but he covered her mouth with his hand. He ran his hand across the smooth expanse of her naked back, down to the rise of her buttocks. He brushed his fingertips against her hardened nipples. He pressed his face into her neck and inhaled the sharp, animal scent of her. She moaned softly and turned onto her back. His fingers traced down across her flat stomach, into the warm, wet crease between her legs.

'Tafara,' she said.

Carefully he got on top of her and her hands took him and guided him. He buried his face in against her flesh and she held onto him.

After, when she was sleeping again, he stood at the door of the hut and gazed out across the village. The sky had begun to clear and the moonlight reflected off the wet thatch. Nothing stirred. Behind the village rose the bulk of the hill, while to the south and east the valley dropped away. His land. The land of his fathers. The land of his children.

Tafara leaned back against the doorpost and smiled.
He had almost forgotten the previous evening.

3

Kristine lifted the child carefully from Natalie's arms, wrapping the thin cloth tightly around its body. With the back of her finger she stroked its tiny cheek and cooed. The baby opened its eyes and began to snivel again, a thin wail that rose into a ferocious complaint causing the dog to look up worried and slink away to a shady corner.

'He's hungry,' Kristine murmured.

'We found him up on the kopje,' Roy commented. 'Lucky Nat has sharp ears, or the poor little thing would have been food for the birds.'

Warmed by her uncle's compliment, Natalie slid down from the back of the horse. She led it around to the stables. In the shadow of the stable block, she paused and leaned in against the side of the horse, pressing her nose against the warm skin of its neck, inhaling its scent. The smell calmed her. Reminded her of being a teenager in Suffolk. She felt her heart slowly calm and the darkness receded. She patted the horse and whispered to it, then turned and gave the reins to one of the stable boys.

The sun was riding high over the hills and the heat had begun to rise and Natalie's shirt clung uncomfortably to her back. Flies were gathering on the dead buck her uncle had shot earlier which Bhekinkosi had taken down off the back of Roy's horse. The flies settled on her skin, too, an irritating prickle on the back of her neck, on the burnt, tender parts of her arms, sticky already with sweat.

Roy wiped his face with a rag and helped Bhekinkosi to hang the buck. Natalie stood a while watching the two men work, the flies buzzing around them. A thin shaft of brilliant sunlight cut through a window and sliced the dark shadows of the barn. Bhekinkosi disappeared into a small room against the back wall.

'Who do you think left the baby there?' Natalie asked.

Roy shrugged. 'Could have been anyone. Some mother with little enough to feed herself. Strange.' He shook his head. 'Can't say I ever heard of such a thing around here.'

'Is it that bad?' Natalie asked. 'That people can't feed themselves?'

'The crops have failed for the last couple of years,' Roy said. He straightened up and wiped his hands on the rag. 'The economy is shot through. If you're a small subsistence farmer, as many are around here, then things have been tough.'

'What are you going to do?'

Roy looked at her. His face was in shadow, but his grey eyes were clear and sharp. Natalie's father had died when she was ten. The image of him was blurred; fractured memories of sitting on his knee, laughing on a beach on the south coast, the rain beating down on them. He had been nothing like Roy. He was a teacher, a gentle man. She wondered what it had been like for her cousin Barbara to have had a father like Roy.

The sunlight lay in thin stripes across the neatly swept floor, and towards the rear of the building an open door illuminated the gloomy belly of the building. Footsteps scuffed on the concrete and Bhekinkosi appeared wiping his face with the back of his arm, a large, sharp knife in his hand.

'Can you take care of this on your own, Bhekinkosi?' Roy asked.

Bhekinkosi nodded languorously.

Roy put a hand to the bottom of his back and stretched his spine, a small wince tightening his features. He walked to the doors of the barn and gazed out across his property towards the road. Past the house, the lawn stretched down towards the gates and, beyond them, past the brilliant blue of the Jacaranda, was the dusty road to Bindura.

'Well,' Roy said finally, 'I don't really know.'

Natalie opened the back door of the large house and took off her riding boots, an old pair of Barbara's, and put on a pair of worn leather slippers her aunt had loaned her. She wished again that her cousin was there. For a moment she stood in the quiet hallway and took a deep breath, collecting herself, and then she slopped down the neat, bright corridor to the kitchen. Kristine was seated at the table, talking. By the sink the maid, a large woman with a flowered dress, held the small baby up in the air jiggling it around and laughing. A thin trail of milk dribbled from the boy's lower lip onto her dress.

'You haven't heard anything?' Kristine asked the maid.

'Not a thing, Ma'am.'

'They could have driven out from Bindura, of course,' Kristine said.

'Who can tell,' the maid said. 'It could have been anyone. She must have been desperate though, to leave such a beautiful baby.'

'He is a beauty,' Kristine commented with a warm smile. She got up from the table and joined her maid by the window, taking the baby from her.

'It's a boy?' Natalie asked.

Kristine laughed. 'Yes, it's a boy. You couldn't tell?'

'I didn't really look,' Natalie muttered, blushing.

The door opened and Roy entered the kitchen. He had changed and washed, his hair slicked back from his face, accentuating the sharp angles of his features. He wore a blue shirt and fawn chinos and looked smart, as if he were back in the Home Counties rather than on a small farm in a rugged valley in Northern Zimbabwe. Walking over to the stove, he poured himself a coffee from the pot that had been warming there, then leant back against the kitchen counter and observed his wife with the baby in her arms.

'What are you going to do?' she asked.

The maid had turned back to the sink, and rinsed the bottle she had fed the baby from. Putting it to dry, she wiped her hands and shuffled away to her room around the back of the kitchen. Roy ran a hand through his hair and sipped from his coffee. He shook his head.

'Shouldn't you call the police?' Natalie asked.

Kristine glanced around at her and then back at Roy. Natalie saw the barely perceptible look that passed between the two of them.

'They're not much use,' Kristine said, after a few moments. 'It probably wouldn't be the best thing.'

'Miriam could take it in,' Roy commented, but he sounded less than convinced.

'I don't think she's any more keen to go there than you are,' Kristine said.

'No,' Roy said. 'You're probably right.'

Natalie was aware of the tension in the air, that there were things unspoken. She wanted to ask, but felt timid. She had flown into Harare three days earlier and her uncle had picked her up from the airport. She had never met Roy and Kristine before; they had immigrated to Africa before she had been born to take over the family farm. Her cousin, Barbara, had visited England the previous year and stayed with Natalie and her mother. Barbara was lively, bright and vivacious and despite being a few years younger than Natalie, they had got on well. Natalie had been looking forward to seeing her, but she had flown down to Cape Town as a part of her university course, Roy told her on the road back to the farm.

Roy and Kristine had been warm and welcoming, but Natalie felt isolated and alone. The first day she had wandered fairly aimlessly around the farm, and then settled with a book in her room. By evening she had felt the dark mood descending upon her, so the next day she helped her uncle with some of the farm work. Her hands, unused to manual labour quickly blistered, and the heat made her head throb. She had excused herself. Her uncle had nodded curtly. 'Of course.'

'Actually,' Roy said, shifting the coffee to his other hand, 'I thought I'd drive down to Pasi. See if anybody there had heard anything. Somebody there would take him, I'm sure.'

Kristine shifted, clutching the baby against her breast. She looked down at it and did not answer for some moments.

'You think that's the best way?'

Roy didn't answer. Draining the coffee cup he placed it next to the sink. He glanced at his watch and then leant over and kissed his wife on the forehead, holding the back of her head tenderly. She closed her eyes and rested her forehead against his chest, the baby between the two of them.

'You can come,' Roy said to Natalie, pulling away from Kristine. 'See something of village life over here.'

Pasi lay on the other side of the range of hills behind the farm. The Land Rover sped down the road away from Bindura and after a few miles turned off onto a dust track at the end of an orchard of orange trees. Behind them a thick plume of dust rose into the hot air, forming a long sandy tail that stretched behind them for half a mile. The road twisted through the dense undergrowth and began to climb up and then duck down between the craggy hills. A dry ravine cut away at the side of the road for a short way then disappeared.

The late morning country seemed deserted. The sun was almost directly above the car and Natalie's blouse clung to her, sodden and uncomfortable. Behind her seat, the baby lay unhappy on a layer of blankets in a wooden box. His cry was scarcely audible above the roar of the engine and the rasp of the tyres on the rough surface of the road.

The village emerged suddenly from behind a copse of

trees; conical, thatch-roofed cottages with baked mud walls, cracked and desolate. Around it stretched small fields. The earth was parched, the crops fading. A malnourished goat trampled the brown grass. The ground was red clay. The road had grown rough and uneven and the Land Rover had been forced to drive slowly, picking its way with care across the gullies and rifts, scars of previous seasons' rains.

The sound of the engine alerted the village and by the time the vehicle reached it half a dozen small children had crowded the doorways, hands stuck in their mouths, wide eyed, half naked, bodies pale from the dust. Behind them, in the shadows, adults lurked, peering out from the gloom at the visitors.

Roy drew to a halt at the edge of the village and killed the engine. The dust settled over the two of them, clogging in the perspiration that slicked their skin. The baby's scream was suddenly loud and insistent, building in waves from an angry gurgle to a full throated bellow, reedy and ferocious. Roy opened the door of the Land Rover and stepped out.

A figure emerged pushing aside the children and stepping out into the dazzling sunlight; a thin man in a brightly patterned shirt, his hair had begun to thin but his beard was full and long; grey and white but with patches, still, of the rich black it must once have been. His feet were bare. He wiped his hands on a dirty cloth and pushed it into his back pocket.

'*Tikukwazisei*,' Roy said, walking over to him.

'*Kwaziwai*,' the man responded flatly.

Seeing Roy, figures emerged from the shadows. The children sloped out nervously and Roy smiled and held out his hand, proffering a sweet to one of the boys. He approached cautiously and took the sweet as if from a tiger.

'Thank you,' he said, and turned and ran.

'Bring the baby,' Roy called to Natalie who had waited by the car.

Pulling out the box she carried it across the parched earth

towards the shade of a large Msasa tree where Roy and the villager had gone. She stroked the cheek of the baby and tried to calm it, but the small face wrinkled with anger and it continued to howl. Women emerged from the huts, curious; an elderly woman, almost bent double, her head wrapped in a scarf, scrutinised her openly.

They squatted in the shade of the tree. One of the women brought drinks and old metal cups on a tray, carefully pouring the tea and adding heaps of sugar before pressing them on Roy and Natalie. The villagers crowded around, at first a little shy, but quickly drawn to the baby in the wooden box. A conversation snapped between them, short, sharp sentences that seemed to be thrown like pebbles. Roy nodded and replied and one of the women plucked the child from the blankets and cradled it warmly to her breast. Almost immediately the baby quietened. Its arms reached up and the woman laughed and tossed another sentence over her shoulder to the other women. She loosened her top and pulled out a large breast, guiding the fat nipple towards the baby's hungry mouth.

'Where did you say you found the child?' the man asked.

'Up on Drew's Kopje, at the back of the farm,' Roy explained. 'We were out riding early and as we came down over the hill the girl heard the sound of it screaming.'

'And there was nobody around?'

'Nobody. We would have seen them. There was no sign of anyone.'

The man grunted. The women assaulted him with a volley of questions and he repeated the story to them in Shona.

'It reminds me of the old tale,' the man said.

The baby suckled greedily from the breast of the woman and the sound of it carried above that of the cicadas and the goat rustling in a pile of rubbish.

'What are you talking about, father?' one of the women said.

'*Kare kare*, long long ago,' the man said, taking on the role of village story teller, his voice clear and loud, 'there was a woman of the village who had developed a taste for the meat of the buck, the *duiker*. She begged her husband for it and would fill herself, not leaving a part of it for the dogs, sucking the very marrow from its bones. One day she went out into the bush and there saw a sleeping hyena with a *duiker* it had killed. 'Give me the *duiker*,' she pleaded with the hyena. 'I'll give you my very child for it.' And so they made their agreement. Later that year the woman became pregnant, and when she had given birth, she forgot all about her promise to the hyena! The hyena did not forget, though.'

He stopped and nodded and looked about him significantly. 'This woman has obviously left her child for the hyena.'

'Father, that is just an old tale,' the woman holding the child laughed.

'Maybe,' the old man nodded. 'But this is an old country.'

Roy spread some American dollar bills on the ground. He counted them out carefully for the man in the flowered shirt. The man nodded, picked them up and counted them himself, carefully, before tucking them into the pocket of his shirt.

'I could take it to the police,' Roy said, 'but there seems little use in that, and…'

'Of course, there is no need to say,' the man interrupted.

'You perhaps could trace the mother. The money is to help look after it.'

'It will help.'

'If you need more…'

'There is no need. It is enough.' The man's attitude was surly. He barely looked at Roy, Natalie noted.

The children had begun to crowd closer to Natalie, giggling and nervous. She smiled and reached out her hand, which made them run and duck for cover behind the women's skirts with squeals of laughter. A girl, on the edge of adolescence, stepped lightly from one of the huts and came to take the children, chiding them and leading them over to sit beneath another tree. The children sat around her obediently. She held her head high, and in a clear voice began to count in English from one to ten. The children chanted after her, the sounds muddled and heavily accented.

'That is Memories,' one of the women said to Natalie as she gazed at the scene. 'She would like to be a teacher. There was a school once, down beyond the village. But the teacher, he has gone now and there is nothing for her. She teaches the children what she can.'

As the Land Rover picked its way carefully back down the deeply rutted lane towards the main road, they sat in silence. Natalie gazed out through the window, at the dry grass and the stunted trees. The sun seemed to lay heavily upon the land, oppressive, hard and unforgiving. The metal of the car was blisteringly hot and the path in front of them shimmered as though dissolving.

'The teacher was arrested,' Roy said. 'He was a supporter of the MDC, an activist. They came one day last year and took him away and nobody has heard from him since.'

'The old man didn't seem very friendly,' Natalie said.

'Moses?' Roy laughed. 'He's always been like that. He's a surly old bugger.'

Natalie was relieved when they got back to the farm. Its tidy, clipped lawns and the low farmhouse with its veranda covered with bougainvillea seemed safe and familiar after the poverty of the village. Roy's dogs ran out to greet the car, barking. Natalie had been given a small cottage around at the back of the farm. It was a one bedroom chalet, with a small sitting room and a kitchen, and views across the back from the grilled patio of the descending hill and the woods on the far slope.

Stripping off her dust-caked clothes she got into the shower, luxuriating in the cool flow of the water. She washed the dust from her hair and wrapped it up in a towel.

Later she sat by the desk and pulled a photograph from her journal and gazed at it for some time. She was about to stand it up against the wall, but then thought better of it. She pulled out a sheet of paper and reached for the blue biro, chewing it thoughtfully. After some minutes, she put it down again and got up and walked over to the patio. Taking a glass of water, she went to sit in the shadow of the wall. Behind the cottage a flame tree blossomed, beautiful orange-red flowers. The lawn stretched down to a low wall; beyond that were Msasa trees and a tall baobab. The road from Bindura was just visible through the leaves.

It was as she was thinking of the girl, Memories, from the village, that she saw the police car approach slowly up the road.

4

It was mid-afternoon when the white men arrived at Tafara's village.

Following the late arrival of the rains there had been a long month of heavy downfalls. The parched earth had been satisfied; the valley was lush and green and the hot, heavy air was alive with insects. The cattle had begun to fatten up in the fields. Tafara had felt the village slowly relax. Despite the uncomfortable weather, the heat and the humidity so intense that sometimes it felt as though you waded in soup, there was a feeling that the curse they had fallen under after the death of Chimukoko had been lifted, that the spirits had been appeased, that disaster had been averted.

The white men arrived on horseback, five of them in khaki uniforms, rifles slung on their backs and belts lined with cartridges, their great hats shading their eyes from the strong sunlight. On a smaller horse, inferior both in stature and health, their black guide rode. He wore an old khaki shirt, a little like that worn by the white men, but it was unbuttoned and beneath it he wore a *nhembe*, a loincloth made from the skin of a goat. It was this man who rushed forward first, as the white men dismounted and looked around the village.

Tafara went out to greet them. He recalled the white men that had visited the village when his father was alive, these men looked different; they were stiffer somehow, taller, proud like warriors.

The children scattered from their games in the centre of the village and hid in the dark shadows of the entrance to the huts, peering out at these pale warriors from between the legs of the women.

The guide spoke Shona with a strange accent, as though he came from some valley far away, down to the south, closer to the Ndebele. He was an interpreter for the British South African Police, he told Tafara, who were scouting the region. The police greeted Tafara with friendly, relaxed smiles and he invited them into the larger hut. The interpreter settled comfortably, happily drinking the beer that was offered him. The white men seemed more uncomfortable, crossing their legs, their backs stiff like rods. One of the white men remained standing by the door to the hut, his rifle resting on the ground. They glanced around with dull curiosity.

The leader of these men seemed to be the broadest of the group. His chest and stomach bulged beneath the khaki uniform. His hair was cut very short, but he had a large beard and moustache that obscured the whole lower part of his face. He glanced into the gourd of beer that had been presented to him and mumbled something to the man beside him and then lay it before his feet. Pulling out a white cloth from his pocket he wiped his face and then began to address Tafara and Kamba who was sat beside him.

He spoke for some time and occasionally their African guide translated, throwing out the odd explanation of the white man's words as he ate and drank.

'Her majesty, the big queen of England… charter… this land, part of the district of Salisbury…'

It meant little to Tafara and he sat quietly contemplating the visitors. The gold prospectors that had visited his father had not been uniformed; they had been armed certainly, but had carried themselves in a different manner. These men made Tafara nervous. They walked with assurance and they spoke to him and to the elders with a familiarity and authority that Tafara did not understand. They did not seem to be petitioning as the previous whites had been.

'Security… stability… ' the translator droned on, between swigs of beer and a mouthful of *sadza*. He spoke Shona as though it was not his mother tongue. It was stilted and ungainly with words in a dialect Tafara did not understand. He speaks like an animal wearing clothes, Tafara thought, he can do it, but it does not seem natural or comfortable. Sometimes, seemingly at a loss as to how he should translate a phrase tossed out by the white man, the translator threw in a word that was not Shona at all.

'The hut tax will be ten shillings. For the elderly and the infirm you do not have to pay -'

'I don't understand,' Tafara interrupted.

'It is payable as you have the means,' the interpreter explained, glancing around the hut, taking it all in. 'You can pay in cattle, or grain, or if these are not available to you then it is possible for you to send somebody from your village to pay in labour.'

'For what am I paying?' Tafara asked, bewildered.

'For the good governance of the region, for the protection offered by the British South African Police and because it is the law.' The interpreter's voice descended from high minded argument to contemptuous statement of fact.

The white men had risen. They left the interpreter with one thin, pale, young policeman who had taken out a pad and noted down the names of each person who lived in the village, while the rest of the group walked around noting the amount of buildings, the grain in the storage and the head of cattle corralled at the edge of the village.

The villagers had gathered and stood gazing at the men suspiciously. Though they did not understand what was going on, the assertive behaviour of the white men worried them. The freedom with which they walked around the village and took note of their possessions, their cattle and defences startled them; and yet they did not seem to be threatening violence. Often they smiled and waved and patted the heads of the children. And then they were gone, their horses ambling off down the track, the interpreter trailing behind them.

The elders of the village gathered at dusk and the mood was dark. Kamba sat to the right of Tafara. He was angry, his face furrowed with deep creases, sharp lines across the fat. Beside him was Ngunzi, who had been a friend of Tafara's father, a thin man with a stooped back, slow of speech, but wise and kind. Mhuru and Mbudzi, younger men, sat further back.

'I have heard of this from other villages,' Kamba growled. 'They demand this tax and take it by force if it is not given willingly.'

'Better to offer a head of cattle and live in peace,' Ngunzi offered quietly.

'And then next time? Another? And another? They will swallow us with their greed. First they came and offered to buy pieces of land. Now, more of them have come, they have arrived in large numbers with their guns and their soldiers and no longer do they want to buy things, they simply come to take them.'

'It is not their land, they will show respect,' Mhuru said.

'What are the others doing?' Tafara asked. 'Those from the other villages you have heard from?'

'What can they do?'

'If we acted together, then the whites would not trouble us. Not just one village, but all the villages united.'

'What you say is right,' Ngunzi said. 'But who could bring this about?'

'I will go up to Nehanda,' Tafara said.

Around him the heads nodded. Kamba slapped a hand on his shoulder and poured out for him a jug of beer.

'Yes,' he said. 'Let us go up to Nehanda.'

5

The police car slowed as it approached Roy Drew's farm. At first Natalie thought it was going to continue, but it turned off the metalled road into the dusty drive and in through the gates, pulling up out of her line of sight, before the farmhouse. The farm was quiet. The afternoon sun lay heavy upon the hills, making movement difficult. The air was still and the blossom on the flame tree was static. As she was watching, a flower fell from the tree and drifted, as if in slow motion, to the dry grass.

She had just picked up a book and was settling in one of the worn armchairs when she heard a timid knock on the cottage door. Bhekinkosi stood outside, stooped slightly, as though embarrassed. He indicated with a flick of his thumb to the main house.

'You are wanted up at the house, Miss.' A bead of perspiration stood out on his forehead and dripped slowly down into the pit of his eye.

Bhekinkosi's nervousness infected Natalie.

'What is it?'

He shook his head. 'I don't know, Miss.'

She put the novel down on the table and followed the young man up the path to the main house. The garden was quiet; the dogs had found refuge in the shade and were sleeping, or lying panting. Pushing open the door, Natalie entered the house, while Bhekinkosi slipped off eagerly around the back towards the barn. From the entrance hall came the sound of voices.

Two policemen in khaki shirts and blue trousers were stood in the hallway. Both wore peaked caps and stood stony-faced. From their belts hung holstered pistols and batons. One of the policemen had been sweating and dark circles spread from beneath his arms. His shirt stuck to a large belly.

Roy had been speaking, but he stopped as Natalie walked in. For a moment there was silence as Natalie surveyed the tableau. Kristine had been crying; the rims of her eyes were red. The blood eased slowly back into Roy's face, so that it was its normal colour by the time he spoke again.

'Natalie,' he said, glancing down at the clean, tiled floor, 'we're going to have to go down to the police station in Bindura to make a statement.'

'Okay,' she replied, feeling her heart thump. 'About what?'

'About the child,' the policeman said, enunciating each word carefully and deliberately.

As Roy indicated for them to move towards the door, clearly eager to see them out of the house, the policemen drew out a pair of handcuffs.

'That's not necessary,' Roy said.

'I decide what is necessary, Mr Drew.'

'For goodness sake, man, what am I going to do? Run away? Assault you?'

Kristine stood stiffly, her back against the wall, her face pale. Natalie felt an icy current run across her skin. The policeman reached out and took hold of Roy's arm, deftly flicking the handcuff closed on his wrist. As he grabbed for the other arm, Roy stood back resisting. Instinctively, Natalie drew her own arms behind her. The second policeman stepped in, grabbing hold of Roy, and for a moment they tussled as Roy fought against the hand being cuffed. The second policeman had begun to sweat and both looked unhappy. As Roy was marched out through the front door, the policeman took hold of Natalie's arm and pulled her after her uncle.

The sudden heat of the sun, after the cool of the large, open entrance hall of the farm, was blistering and seemed to radiate from the patrol car squatted on the gravel in front of the house. Some of the farm workers had come out and lingered at a distance as Natalie and Roy were pushed into the back of the car.

Inside the car seemed hotter than it had been outside. When Natalie rested her bare arm against the metal of the door, it burned her skin, leaving an angry red line. As the car turned, Natalie saw Kristine stood in the darkness, just inside the door. Roy saw her too and attempted a smile. The car did a sharp turn, driving up over the neat lawn, and accelerated hard so that dust and grit clouded the entrance to the farm.

The windscreen of the police car was cracked, a jagged fork rising from the driver's corner right to the middle. The springs seemed to have gone in the back seat, so that at every pothole Natalie's teeth rattled and her whole body jarred. Beside her Roy was silent, gazing out across the neat fields of the farm as they drove down the road towards Bindura.

Neither of the policemen spoke and the only sound was an occasional crackly message on the radio. Once the policeman in the passenger seat picked up the receiver and began to speak. Twice he repeated himself, the second time with irritation, before slamming it back into its holder and muttering something before he too turned to gaze out across the passing country.

When they had left the Drew farm behind, the country to each side of the road became less cultivated. Overgrown fields and orchards, rotting farmyards, and redundant machinery rusting away among the weeds.

'This farm here,' Roy said, loudly, indicating the plain to the north, 'used to belong to my friend Nigel Heseltine. Two hundred acres given over to coffee and tobacco. He employed one hundred locals. Look at it now.' The fields were thick with brush, saplings grew in a spindly fashion along with bushes and thick, dry grass. He shook his head.

'What are they doing now?' Roy addressed the two policemen. 'Those families? What are they doing now?'

'They have found better jobs,' the policeman said.

'Better jobs?' Roy laughed. 'Rubbish. There are no jobs. They're starving, that's what's happening to them now.'

'They have much better jobs now,' the policeman in the passenger seat asserted. He half turned, grinning. 'Before they were oppressed, they were treated no better than cattle. Now they are free and have good jobs that pay them well and treat them like decent humans.'

'Is that why they come up to my farm begging then?' Roy Drew's face was growing red. A vein throbbed at his temple. 'Is that why they come up imploring me for any work I can give them?'

The policeman turned back to stare through the windscreen.

'Nigel ran a good farm,' Roy continued, 'it was profitable. He paid taxes to the government. His workers had jobs and were paid decent wages and could feed their families.'

The policeman whipped around, his arm shooting out, pressing the pistol into Roy's chest. Roy leaned forward, his handcuffed hands raised, his cheeks tight and almost purple. Natalie grabbed hold of her uncle's arm. The blood had drained from her own face, and she could feel her heart pumping hard somewhere up near her throat.

'Uncle Roy…'

The two men stared at each other, loathing etched deeply in their faces, eyes sharp with bitterness. Spittle flecked Roy's lips. The policeman's eyes narrowed and slowly he withdrew the pistol and put it back into its holster on his hip. He laughed and shook his head. Roy fell back against the seat and closed his eyes. Natalie could see her uncle's chest rising and falling as he attempted to control his anger.

Natalie withdrew her hand and found that it was shaking. She clasped her hands together and leaned her head against the dirty padding behind the window and watched as the desolate country rolled past.

The police station was a basic building, divided into a number of unattractive rooms, sparsely furnished. Tattered curtains hung between the main reception area and a side office. They were seated on a low bench against the wall and told to wait. Roy leaned back, his head against the wall, his hands still secured with the handcuffs.

'I'm sorry about the outburst,' he said.

Natalie nodded. She kept her eyes down. A number of policemen wandered around, occasionally glancing down at the two of them. The two arresting officers had disappeared. The police station smelled of sweat and dust and something more acrid that Natalie couldn't place.

'Just tell them what happened,' Roy said to her.

'About what?' Natalie asked desperately.

'About the child. The baby. Don't try to hide anything. Somebody has obviously reported it already anyway so there'd no point in pretending.'

'Who do you think reported it?'

Roy shook his head. 'Who knows? Somebody from the village? Unlikely I would think, so that would mean somebody from the farm.'

'One of your employees?'

Roy didn't answer. His eyes were closed. His face was calmer now, but set hard. He did not move when the policeman who had arrested them came out and called his name. Two policemen grabbed his arms and pulled him to his feet and pushed him through the curtain into the office beyond. The curtain fell back down so that Natalie could see nothing. Chair legs scuffed against the concrete floor.

The remaining policeman stood up.

'You come here,' he said to Natalie, indicating a door on

the opposite side of the station.

Two other men were waiting for Natalie there, one seated behind a rough wooden desk, the other leaning against a wall. One was uniformed, a large man in his forties, with glasses and fingers like sausages. The man leaning against the wall was in casual clothes, brown trousers and a pale shirt. A single chair stood before the desk and the policeman pushed Natalie down into it, before turning and leaving.

The large policeman looked at her, a supercilious gaze down the length of his stubby nose. His fingers tapped lightly against the wood.

'Passport,' he said.

Natalie fumbled in her pocket and pulled out her passport, placing it on the table top. The policeman picked it up and flicked through it, coming to rest on the final page with her information on. His eyes flicked lazily between the photo and Natalie, as though he suspected it may be a fake. Finally he dropped it down and rubbed the rolls of his face.

'What are you doing here, Miss Chambers?'

'I'm on holiday.'

'Holiday? You go to Paris on holiday, or Rome. Why would you come to this little, dusty town for your holiday?'

Unsure how to respond, or indeed whether it had been a question, Natalie said nothing. The policeman observed her. She heard the non-uniformed policeman behind her stir.

'How long are you here for?'

'I hadn't quite decided,' Natalie said.

'Haven't decided? You said this was a holiday.'

'Yes.'

'A holiday from what?'

Again Natalie felt unsure how she was expected to respond. The policeman's tone had shifted from ironic to cold. Natalie felt a bead of sweat slip down from her hairline and rest in her eyebrow. She reached up and wiped it away.

'I'm not sure what you mean,' she said finally. 'Roy is my uncle. I needed to get some space, a bit of time to forget about things.' She looked up at him, as though he might understand. He stared back at her, eyes hard. 'I just came here to get away,' she said weakly.

'Tell me about the money,' the policeman said, shifting back in his seat, his hands folding over his stomach.

'What money?'

'How much money did Drew give them?'

For some moments Natalie searched to follow the logic of the questions. Her mind flipped back over the proceeding days and tried to pin down what she might know about money. There had been money, she thought, but where?

'Money?' she said, hoping the policeman might change track again.

A firm hand grabbed her shoulder and spun her around. Natalie almost cried out. The plain-clothed officer gripped her hard and brought his face close to Natalie's so that she could smell the man's breath, stale from cigarette smoke and beer.

'We know Drew handed over money this morning. How much did he give?'

The village, she thought. Of course. To pay for the care of the child. She recalled it now; the dollar notes spread on the dusty earth.

'I don't know,' Natalie said. She wasn't sure how much she should say, she didn't want to incriminate her uncle. But she recalled Roy's words; tell them what happened. There's no point pretending.

'There was maybe fifty dollars.'

'Fifty American dollars?'

Natalie nodded. 'About that.'

'And you,' the policeman said, leaning forward. 'How much money did you bring to Zimbabwe?'

Natalie hesitated. She had to declare her money when she came through customs and she hadn't wanted to let the immigration authorities know how much she was bringing, particularly as they seemed so keen for her to change it into the worthless Zimbabwean dollars.

'About five hundred pounds,' she said cautiously.

'Have you seen one of these?'

The policeman produced a card, which he held out to Natalie. She looked at it, but the policeman indicated for her to take it. In orange letters it read *Membership Card*, and beneath that was a logo featuring the Zimbabwean bird and the words *Movement for Democratic Change MDC*. As she took the card, Natalie heard a commotion from behind her. She half turned to look but the plain-clothed officer blocked her view.

'Your uncle has one of these, yes?'

Natalie shook her head. Her brain was whirring, beginning to put things in place, to suddenly understand the logic of the questioning.

'No,' Natalie said. 'I've never seen one of these before.'

'Your uncle is a member of the MDC,' the policeman told her.

'I don't know about that,' she said.

The noise from the other room had quietened.

'This morning,' the policeman said, 'you went with your uncle to pay one of their activists. He supports them. He bank-rolls them.' The policeman seemed to like this term. He turned it on his tongue, and then repeated it. 'This is just a friendly little chat,' he said then. He grinned, hitching his holster up into Natalie's line of vision. 'Just a little warning. Paris is nice. You should go there on holiday. Or Rome. You're a young woman, what is there for you here?'

When Roy moved out into the sunlight he held his head high, his chest out and stepped vigorously as though on a mission to get somewhere. Only outside the station, with Natalie a few steps behind him, did his pace falter and he glanced around and seemed for a moment lost. When he turned, Natalie noticed for the first time the red welt across his cheek bone. Before she had chance to say a word, Roy had turned again and pointed down towards the end of the street.

'There will be a taxi we can hail down there.'

They walked in silence, Roy setting a brisk pace, kicking up small plumes of dust along the street. Natalie struggled to keep up with him. At the corner they stopped. A number of taxis were lined in haphazard fashion along the pavement and Roy approached one and quickly bartered a price he was happy with. In the taxi, Roy didn't speak for a long time. He sat gazing out of the window at the dusty town and then the open fields, at the men and women who walked by the sides of the roads, at the small fires that filled the air with the pungent scent of wood smoke.

'Were you all right?' he asked finally, turning to look at her.

Natalie nodded.

'I'm sorry that you got dragged into all this,' he said. 'Your mother will be furious with me.'

Natalie laughed. 'I've travelled, Uncle Roy. It's not the first time I've got into a scrape.'

'No, but I got you into this one,' he said ruefully. 'Normally it's me having to hold Barbara back. She's the hot-headed one. She's a real Drew. Fiery, Scottish blood.'

Natalie laughed.

'Your mother was the same when she was young.' Roy looked at her. 'Barbara reminds me of her. I bet she hasn't told you that. She was the wild one when we were children, always getting into some kind of problem.'

Natalie tried to imagine her mother in trouble. It was true she occasionally had a sharp tongue and wicked sense of humour, but she had never seen her mother as anything other than a quiet, supportive presence. It was partly to get away from her suffocating concern that Natalie had decided to run away to this farm in northern Zimbabwe. She needed the space. She needed to deal with things on her own and neither Lawrence nor her mother helped with that.

'What did they ask you?' Roy asked.

'They told me you were a member of the MDC,' Natalie

said. 'And that the money you gave them in the village this morning was to support them.'

Roy laughed an ironic snort, short and angry.

'Watch what you say to Kristine,' he said later. 'She has enough to worry about.'

It grew dark early. The sun sank rapidly, and the day disappeared so suddenly that it was still a shock to Natalie to walk out and find that it was already night. They had a quiet dinner in the main house and then Natalie withdrew to the small cottage. The air hummed with the noise of the small generator and the throb of the cicadas. She went to sit out on the patio to enjoy a drink looking down over the grass to the flame tree and the Msasas, but the mosquitoes swarmed in thick clouds and she was soon driven indoors, securing the door and windows tightly.

Sitting at the writing desk, she pulled out the photograph and leaned it against the wall. For some moments she looked at the man who stood beside her in the picture. And then her eyes drifted to her own figure and a wave of sadness washed over her. She felt, suddenly, very alone. Glancing around the small room, she acted decisively.

Pulling her suitcase from the top of the wardrobe she emptied the drawers, piling her clothes neatly back where they had come from, pulling her blouses from their hangers in the wardrobe and packing her books in the side pockets of the case.

She took out her passport and laid it on top.

6

Tafara left the village just as the light began to filter across the sky and the sun was about to rise, a bleary copper colour. He had left Anokosha sleeping, bending over her to inhale one last time the scent of her. She stirred and looked up and smiled, but he closed her eyes.

'Sleep,' he said.

He turned back once only as he crested the hill to look at the houses down in the village. They looked, to him, suddenly so fragile. Clouds gathered darkening his spirit. He turned, then, towards Nehanda's village which was a two day walk away.

He cut south below the range that swooped in a semi-circle across the land; high forested hills, with sharp granite escarpments, and narrow valleys, dark and forbidding. The hills were littered with caves where wild animals and spirits lived. They were the home of *n'angas*; of spirit mediums, holy and feared and of tribes friendly and hostile.

Tafara set a steady pace. In a small pouch he carried smoked meat and, over his shoulder, a skin filled with water. From his belt hung a *banga*, a long knife, its blade sharpened to a keen edge, sharp enough to slice the skin as if it was gossamer thin.

A few years earlier he had travelled this route with his

father. On that journey they had come across the occasional settlement of bedraggled and hungry white men, their huts built in the local fashion with thatched roofs and walls daubed with mud. Often the huts were surrounded by covered wagons. These settlers had been thin, their feet badly shod and their cattle emaciated or dying. They had been making their way into the hills looking for gold in the depleted mines of the ancients. Desperate men, eyes burning with determination, or perhaps just greed. They tried to barter with the Shona tribes, but had little to offer beyond beads and calico.

These same settlements had expanded now and the houses were more substantial, built from stone. More like small forts. Occasionally on the top of a tall pole a brightly coloured cloth flew. The land around them had been turned into farmland and the whites looked healthier. In the fields there were occasionally white women.

As the sun rose higher he paused to drink from the goat skin. He rested for some moments, squatting in the shade of a Msasa tree. He had seen Nehanda before; his father had taken him to consult with her when he had been a small boy. Though Nehanda was not old, she was called *Mbuya* by everyone, grandmother, the traditional title given to a spirit medium. She was a fairly thickset woman who stood with noble up-rightness, a large nose and sad eyes. Her voice when she spoke was direct and sharp. She lived in a cave, in Mazoe.

Nehanda was a *mudzimu*, an ancestral spirit, the incarnation of the daughter of Mutota, the first king of the Monomatapa kingdom. Mutota had ordered his daughter to sleep with her brother and from them, through this incest ritual, great power emanated. The spirit of this great princess lived on in Nehanda. People would travel from miles around to ask for her advice, to listen to her teaching, to request that she intercede with Mwari, the great God, on their behalf. Particularly over the last few years as the cattle had died in increasing numbers and the crops failed.

At the end of the first day, Tafara rested away from the road, in the shade of a large rock. He built a small fire to keep away the animals and ate some of the meat. He lay down, resting his head on a granite stone and, weary from the long day's walk, fell asleep quickly. He had been dreaming of a young girl bathing in a stream, when he was suddenly awoken.

The last light of day had long faded from the sky. The moon had risen and the hills were bathed in a ghostly light. His fire had burned low and he shifted over to it, feeding it with some dry wood he had gathered earlier. Sitting up, he hugged his knees. He tried to recall the dream; it had made him feel good, but it melted away as he tried to lay hold on it. In the distance he heard a crackle. The sky was clear. He listened carefully. The noise disturbed him. He tried to remember where he had heard such a sound before, sharp tight cracks, rapid and loud, drifting down the long valley.

He moved early, as soon as the sky began to lighten, determined to reach Nehanda's cave before the day was finished. He had only travelled a few miles, though, when he noticed a figure in the half-light. He hesitated, glancing around to see if there were others close by. A couple of hundred metres away, down the slope on a verdant patch of the valley floor was the stone built farm of the whites. It lay still in the early morning light.

The figure was inert, face down at the edge of the track, half-hidden by a bush. Creeping closer he saw it was a man, dressed in a goatskin loincloth. His legs were twisted oddly.

Bending down, Tafara saw the small hole in his back, almost directly between the shoulder blades. A small clean, circular hole from which blood had oozed. It was dry now. Insects ranged over the body. Though he could see no one, he had the feeling that he was being watched, as though a wild beast was lurking in the dark brush waiting to jump out upon him. But it had been no wild beast that killed this man. Tafara hurried on. He walked fast and as the sun began to descend, he saw its light reflecting in the lake below Nehanda's cave.

On the valley floor, below the cave, was a small village. A cluster of thatched huts on a low rise. A blue haze of wood smoke hung above the roofs catching the last of the day's light as Tafara approached. Groups of men sat around fires, talking. He squatted down, greeting the young men. Their accents were slightly different to his own and he guessed that they were from the south.

The men greeted him, moving apart to allow him to sit.

'It is not possible anymore,' a wiry young man said, continuing the conversation he had interrupted. 'They are taking everything.'

'That is so,' another agreed. 'First they wanted to trade, then more of them came, with their warriors. Then they started to demand we pay taxes.'

'They are bleeding us.'

'Why do you not refuse to give to these men?' Tafara asked.

The men looked at him.

'If you refuse them they come and take what they want,' a small, pot-bellied man said sullenly. '*Mbuya*, Nehanda told us. She said not to be afraid of them, that they have only come to trade. We should offer them one of our best cattle, and say, "We greet you with this meat." She said that should have been enough for them.'

'But it is not,' another broke in. He was an older man with white hair and a grizzled face. 'They came with their guns and they took some of our young men to work on their farms and in their mines as labourers.'

'They are taking good land too.'

'And now the cattle are dying and they blame us, though it is obviously them that have brought the curse of Mwari on our land. Did you hear what happened to Chief Chiweshe? When he failed to slaughter his cattle as they ordered him to do, they took him and they flogged him, before a crowd.'

For some moments there was silence around the fire as

they digested this ignominy. The old men shook their heads. The small man rubbed his belly. They talked on for a long time that night, sharing stories of the white settlers. Tafara listened. Darkness fell across the village. The light of the fire threw shadows up against the walls of the huts. It was a clear and cool night and later, Tafara found a quiet corner and slept dreamlessly.

He was woken early the next morning by the sound of people moving around. Before long he joined the procession out of the village and up over the foothills and onto the mountain. They trailed the goat path cut in the brush, following the curve of the slope up, as it grew in steepness, and the brush became less dense and the trees dropped away beneath them. Turning, the view stretched for miles across the lake and the woodland. The sun had risen and steam rose from the damp earth.

Mbuya Nehanda's cave was high on the mountain. As the procession grew close, Tafara looked up and saw her standing on a lip of rock gazing out across the land. For a moment he paused and observed her; she seemed unaware of the crowd of people winding up the steep path. As he watched she raised her arms to the sun, and the light caught her and she seemed all at once ablaze. Several of the men in the group dropped to the earth and began to mutter her name and to pray for the blessing of Mwari.

When they had assembled, Nehanda addressed them. Her voice was quiet, but heavy with authority. She enunciated each word carefully, as though recalling the voices of those she had heard in her dreams, taking care not to forget or mistake the prophecies tendered to her.

'They are strangers in our land,' she said, 'and it was our duty to welcome them and offer them peace. But they have trampled over our land and they have dug in many places and have not respected the spirits that dwell among us.'

Tafara had squatted in the shade of a rock and listened

intently. He wished his father was beside him now, remembering these words to take them back faithfully to the village.

'When we walk we respect the shadows,' Nehanda continued. 'We know that our land is governed by the spirits of those who have been before us; before we settle our homes we ask for the blessing of the spirits, when we dig wells, when we gather the fruits of the earth we honour the shadows that remind us of who we are and where we are from. These strangers have no knowledge of our land or our spirits. They trample them as they trample our people.

'First they came for the gold, now they hunger for our land and for our young men. Their greed is insatiable and they will not be content until they have sucked the marrow from our bones, and the spirits have been driven from their ancestral homelands.'

She was silent for some moments. She had been gazing up into the air, but now she looked down at the assembled crowd. She examined each man before her. For a moment, Tafara felt her eyes upon him. He squirmed under her scrutiny.

'The time has come for us to repel them,' she said.

'Fan out through the forests and the mountains,' she said. 'Take spears and your *bakatwa*, your sacred weapons. Your ancestors will protect you from the guns of the white strangers, their bullets will turn to water and harm you no more than the rain. Bloody your spears. The time has come.'

Tafara felt his belly burning. He was not a violent man, but he felt a flame kindled inside him. As he listened to the words of Nehanda he felt the spirits awaken and swirl around him. Later there was music, drumming. A *n'anga*, dressed in the skin of a lion called for the blessings of the spirits and they drank millet beer brewed by the women.

During his stay at Nehanda's village the weather had been clear and bright, but large, dark clouds had bubbled up from the east threatening rain as Tafara hurried back, the fire still burning inside him. The elders of the village gathered in the chief's hut and seated themselves to listen to the words of Nehanda. The air was hot and heavy. Tafara's face glowed with perspiration as he told them of his journey, of the white farmsteads, of the stories of the men he had met in Nehanda's village and then of the ascent to see her and to listen to her message.

'They will not be content until they have sucked the marrow from our bones,' he recounted, the words singing in his brain. All his fear that he would forget the message had disappeared when he listened to her. He would never forget those words or the way that she had spoken. 'They have driven the spirits of our ancestors from this land. Rise up and repel them. Fan out through the forests. Their guns will not hurt you; their bullets will turn to water and harm you no more than the rain.'

When he paused and glanced around at the faces, his own eyes burning, the sound of the rain hummed against the thatched roof of the hut. Mhuru and Mbudzi gazed at him, tense with excitement. Kamba nodded his head. Only Ngunzi seemed unsettled.

'War is a heavy burden,' he said. 'It is not something we should rush towards. Far better that we live in peace with our neighbours.'

'But it is not possible to live at peace with the white men,' Mhuru said, his voice tight with frustration. 'They want to enslave us, to take away our land.'

'*Chikomo, shata divi, rimwe ritambire pwere*. One side the hill may be difficult, but on the other side children play,' Ngunzi replied. 'The white men may be difficult, but they may bring blessings too.'

'What blessings? Will taking our land be a blessing to us? Or enslaving us in their mines?'

Silence descended inside the hut. Outside the rain ran from the roofs and hissed against the earth. Thunder rumbled around the valley. Ngunzi was the eldest in the village and had been a close friend of Tafara's father; he had been his teacher and was much respected. Tafara knew that to argue against him and side with the young men would be disrespectful and would seem hot-headed.

'Nehanda has called us to it,' was all that he would say.

For some days after that life in the village continued as it had. One of the cattle had begun to grow thin, and the men slaughtered it fearfully. Cattle-plague had been ravaging the herds on the plains of Mashonaland. So far their valley had seen little of it, but all around herds had fallen sick, dying in a matter of months. A few days later a second cow showed signs of the disease, developing a fever and diarrhoea. Tafara watched helplessly as the animal gave in.

It was the day the second cow died that the white men reappeared. Five policemen on horseback, smartly dressed in uniform with a number of Shona warriors. The translator, the same one they had met previously, approached them with the warriors, while the white mounted police remained at the edge of the village.

'We have come to collect the hut tax,' the translator told them, in his heavily accented Shona.

'We have no tax for you,' Tafara told him sullenly. 'Our cattle have begun dying and we have little enough to survive on ourselves.'

The translator grunted. He turned back to the men on their horses and stammered something in the white man's tongue. The white man sighed. He gave a curt command – his pale eyes glancing around the assembled crowd in the centre of the village.

One of the warriors stepped forward. He pointed his spear towards Mhuru who was seated behind Tafara. 'We will take this one as a labourer.'

'No,' Tafara said, standing up.

'And this one.'

The warriors moved forward, six armed men quickly

overpowering Tafara. They grabbed Mhuru and pulled him away kicking and protesting. They also grabbed Ngunzi's grandson, a tall, thin boy who looked older than his thirteen seasons. From her place among the women they pulled Anokosha, who screamed and looked about desperately for help. Tafara shouted out but as he tried to approach them, the warriors threatened him with their spears.

Tafara approached the white men on their horses. The first wore a peaked cap. His face was sun-reddened and his eyes an icy blue.

'You can't take them,' Tafara protested. 'If you want to take somebody, take me.'

The white man coughed up a mouth of phlegm and spat in Tafara's face. He felt it seeping down his skin as the white men turned and rode away. The warriors forced the captives into a run. Tafara began to run after them, but Ngunzi held him back.

'They will just take you too,' he said.

Anokosha did not turn back to look at the village as they led her away.

7

Natalie woke the next morning her skin sticky with sweat. The bed sheets were knotted uncomfortably around her legs. She stumbled across to the shower and stood for a long time beneath the water, delighting in the cool flow of it through her hair and across her skin. A small window opened from the bathroom looking down over the back of the farm towards the Msasa trees and Natalie gazed out at the beautiful view as she showered. One of the farm workers was cutting the grass, slowly, methodically with a primitive scythe.

On the chair by her bed her suitcase was packed. For some moments, the towel wrapped loosely around her, she regarded the luggage as if unsure, which was not actually the case. The first emotion she had felt upon opening her eyes that morning had been of relief that she had made the decision to go back home to England. The only thing that made her hesitate was the thought of telling her aunt and uncle after all they had done for her. A part of her, too, did not like the sense of defeat; that she was going home so quickly.

Stepping across to the writing table she picked up the photograph she had left there. Once again she looked at it closely, examined the image of the two young people. Gently, she stroked with the tip of her finger the belly of the woman scarcely visible beneath the loose cotton shirt. Her heart squeezed painfully. She tucked the picture inside the flap of her case and, after taking out some clothes for her journey, zipped it up, dressed and sat on the edge of the bed.

She was startled by a knock on the door. One of the boys who lived on the farm was stood outside. He wore a long shirt that was creased and dirty and short trousers, frayed around the knees. He could have been no older than seven or eight, Natalie thought. She smiled, but the child looked petrified. When the boy said nothing, Natalie bent down to his level.

'Is everything okay?' she asked.

The boy nodded mutely. He pointed behind him, towards the fence along the edge of the property that bordered the road to Bindura.

'What is it?' Natalie asked. Immediately she felt the flow of adrenaline. She calmed herself. 'What did you want?'

'There is somebody that wants to speak to you,' the boy said, then, solemnly.

'Who?' Natalie said. 'Who wants to speak to me?'

The boy shook his head. 'I cannot say.'

Natalie got back to her feet. She glanced over towards the fence, her brain working fast. Was it some kind of trap? Who could want to see her?

'Well if you can't say, then I'm not going to go,' Natalie said to the boy, a little impatiently.

'She told me I couldn't say anything,' the boy said glumly, hanging his head in an almost exaggerated scene of embarrassment.

'She?'

The boy said nothing more. He pointed towards the fence again then turned on his heel and quickly ran away, around the side of the main house towards the small houses of the domestic staff. Natalie followed the direction the boy had pointed and tried to make out any sign of a figure behind the shrubbery and hedge; she could see nothing.

Closing the door, she walked cautiously across the lawn, beneath the shade of the trees towards the road. Behind her she could hear the slow hiss of the scythe as it fell through the dry grass. In the trees the birds chattered and the slow pulse of the cicadas gave the day its rhythm. She stopped a moment, close to the shrubbery, listening carefully for the sound of movement on the other side.

Before her was a Glory Lilly, its leaves succulently green, expansive, spreading up the hedge, its flowers, newly budded, a glorious delicate deep pink with inward curling petals, its scent, honey sweet, hanging heavily upon the air. 'One tenth of an ounce of its root,' her uncle had said a few days before, when they were wandering around the property, 'could kill you outright.' The thought came back to her now, perversely, as she stood listening for her visitor.

Moving close to the fence, she glanced over and at first saw nothing. The fence was chest high, and as it was difficult to approach, she could not get a very good view. For some moments she thought perhaps the boy had been having some kind of joke at her expense, or that perhaps whoever had wanted her had wandered off, and she was about to turn away, when a head rose before her.

For some moments she did not recognise the face.

The girl was perhaps twelve years old. She wore a red sleeveless shirt, with white braiding, and a blue dress from which the pocket had been half torn. Though thin, she looked healthy, and between her parted lips, Natalie noticed a beautiful row of teeth, white and straight. She did not smile, rather she looked at Natalie seriously, her noble face perfectly still and clear except for the slight crinkling of her forehead between her eyes.

'You're from the village,' Natalie said, trying to remember her name. She was sure she had been told it. Vividly she recalled the girl leading the children away to sit beneath the tree and play at school. The girl nodded. When she didn't speak Natalie tried again. 'The little boy said you wanted to speak to me.'

'Yes,' she said.

She examined Natalie boldly and Natalie felt a little uncomfortable under the scrutiny.

'Perhaps I should come around there so we can talk a little more comfortably,' she said.

'Will you be our teacher?'

Natalie gaped. The girl stood on the grass on the other side of the fence, close to the road. Her hands hung by her sides, neither limp, nor tense. She moved from one foot to the other, not turning her eyes from her for a moment.

'Your teacher?'

'We have no one to teach us. Our last teacher was arrested, and now we have no school. With no school there is no chance that I can go to university. Will you be our teacher?'

'Listen I… ' Natalie regarded the girl, bewildered. She did not know how to respond. She could not say that she was not a teacher, as she was. She pictured the girl seated beneath the Msasa tree with the little children gathered around her. Recalled the beaten squalor of the village.

'But I can't,' she said.

The girl gazed at her. The early morning heat was already oppressive and Natalie felt a bead of sweat ease its way down her spine. She ran a hand through her hair.

'You don't want to?'

'It's not that.' Natalie shifted uneasily. 'Look, I'll come round,' she said. 'It's impossible trying to speak over this hedge.'

To get out she had to follow the path around the house, out through the gate beneath the Jacaranda and onto the road. It took her a couple of minutes and she feared that when she got around the girl would be gone, but as she emerged onto the dusty verge of the road she saw her stood there still, gazing across the hedge towards the bungalow just as she had left her. The girl turned when she heard Natalie and watched as she approached.

'We have no one to teach us,' she said again, as Natalie came close to her. Her bearing was proud and her chin tilted back slightly and there was no change in the expression on her face, but Natalie felt there was the slightest hint of desperation in her voice. Of disappointment. 'I want to go to university to study to be a teacher,' the girl said, the words blurting out of her now, 'so that I can come back to the village to teach the children.'

Natalie nodded. She crouched down close to the girl, squatting in the dust. The girl stood above her, looking down into her eyes.

'We used to have a teacher from England,' the girl explained, 'when I was small. But then he went home. After that we had another teacher. He was from Gweru. He was a good teacher and he taught me how to count and to say my alphabet and to write and read.'

She bent down suddenly then and with her finger began to write in the dirt at the side of the road. She formed beautiful neat letters. A tidy, careful script. At first Natalie thought she was writing out the alphabet, but soon she realised the letters spelt out a painstaking sentence. *She walks in beauty like the night.*

'Byron?'

'Our teacher taught us the poem.'

She clasped her hands before her and, casting her eyes up towards the sky, began to declaim the poem. Natalie gazed up at her astonished. She did not falter and told it through to the end. When she had finished, her hands dropped back down to the side of her skirt, and she glanced down at Natalie, and Natalie thought she saw the hint of a smile at the edges of the girl's lips.

'That was very impressive,' she conceded.

'But now we have no teacher,' the girl said, her face suddenly solemn again.

'Listen,' Natalie said. 'I'm going home. I'm going back to England. I'm sorry.'

The disappointment was apparent in her face. Her shoulders, which had been held beautifully high and proud, slumped slightly.

'I'm sorry,' Natalie said again.

'You don't like it here?'

'It's very beautiful here,' she said.

'So why are you going home?'

Natalie shook her head and stood up, brushing the dust from the seat of her jeans.

'I don't know,' she said. 'It's difficult here.'

She looked at the girl and her words seemed inadequate. The girl did not respond. She gazed at Natalie evenly and it was hard for her to read what she might be thinking.

'I'm sorry,' the girl said.

She turned and walked away, down the road from Bindura, back towards her village. It had taken twenty minutes to make the drive in the Land Rover, though it was true that part of the journey, down the final track towards the village, they had driven little quicker than walking pace. It must have taken the girl at least an hour, if not longer to have walked to the farm. Natalie watched her as she walked, a steady pace along the edge of the road, her bare feet kicking up the dust. The road shimmered, and soon the girl's body seeped liquid into the waves of heat rising up from the tarmac.

Memories, she thought. That was her name. She turned back to the farm.

Kristine was cheerful when Natalie entered the kitchen. She had lain out breakfast on the large wooden table and the family gathered around it. Natalie felt unable to eat, not even the fruit that Kristine pressed on her. The chatter continued, good-natured banter and laughter. The bruise on Roy's face was blue, but neither he nor Kristine seemed to be bothered by it and no mention was made of the incident the day before. It was as though it had not happened at all. Natalie felt like shouting at them. How could they just ignore the brutality, the bullying?

'I was thinking…' Natalie began as they cleared the table. 'Perhaps I'll be going back home.'

Her voice trailed off. Kristine paused half way to the sink while Roy glanced up at her. Natalie looked down at her hands. Roy nodded slowly, Kristine's face moved barely perceptibly, almost as though she was about to smile but decided not to.

'When were you thinking of going?' Roy asked.

'Well I need to check when the flights are,' Natalie said. She paused. 'Today, if there is a flight.'

Roy nodded and stood up. He took the plates and delivered them to the sink where the maid was stood looking out of the window, obviously listening to the conversation. He touched Kristine's arm, a gentle, tender caress. She glanced up at him and half smiled and turned away.

'Okay,' Roy said. 'Kristine will call the airport and see when the next flight is and if they have any seats. I'll drive you there if they have something available.'

In her bungalow, Natalie slumped glumly down on the end of the bed. She felt as if she had let her aunt and uncle down. She felt, too, as though she was running away at the first hint of trouble and it made her feel like a coward. She felt homesick and longed for the dull normality of her life in England: work, the trip to the pub on a Friday night. And Lawrence. She missed him. There had been a time when the thought of him had hurt her, when she could not bear to see him for what he reminded her of, for what she had lost. But she missed the sound of his voice, the closeness of him. His touch. Being touched.

The idea of staying in Zimbabwe filled her with apprehension and she found the heat oppressive. She lay back on the bed and gazed up at the ceiling. A mosquito had managed to slip in and darted around with a high-pitched whine, reminding her of the need to take her malaria tablets.

She thought of Memories, recalled her standing by the side of the road, in the dust, reciting Byron. She pictured the quiet intensity of her gaze and of the disappointment so clear on her face when she had told her that she was going back to England. She recalled how Memories had taken the children out beneath the Msasa trees and attempted to teach them, remembered the poverty of the village, the running sores on the faces of the little children. The rounded bellies.

She was interrupted by a knock on the door. As she sat up her aunt opened the door and smiled at her. It was a sad smile, she thought, but perhaps she was imagining that.

'There is a plane tomorrow morning,' she said to her. 'I need your passport to call them back and arrange you a seat.'

8

The white men's stockade was a two-day walk to the south. Tafara and another of the young men from the village trekked out to it to try and discover what had happened to Anokosha, Mhuru and the other villager they had taken. For three days they waited outside the walls of the fort with a ragged camp of other men and women from the villages, but they could learn nothing. When their food ran out they returned to the village.

Dark, bilious clouds massed in the normally clear skies. The rivers ran fast making any travel difficult and the water poured from the rocks and washed away the loose top soil and damaged the roofs of the houses, so that they were continually forced to repair them.

Ngunzi sat most days in silence in the entrance to his hut, gazing out across the plains towards the far side of the valley, which often disappeared as another curtain of rain was drawn across the land. Tafara said little to him, nodding as he passed in the morning on his way out into the fields to look after the cattle.

More of the cattle had died. As much as they tried to care for them, there seemed to be little they could do to stop the spread of the disease. The first symptoms would be a heightened temperature in the cattle and a loss of appetite.

Soon after the nasal passages and mouth broke out in sores and then diarrhoea set in. Within a week the animal would be dead. As soon as they spotted symptoms they would isolate the cow and slaughter it, but nothing they did seemed to protect the others.

'Tafara.' Ngunzi called him one evening as he returned to the village.

Tafara stopped. He had slept little in the previous few days and had worked for hours on end. All of his muscles ached and his whole body was so weary that he sometimes caught himself sleeping as he walked. He squatted down at the entrance to Ngunzi's hut.

'Nothing has been heard from Mhuru,' Ngunzi said. 'Or from Anokosha.'

Tafara was not sure whether it was a question or statement, so he said nothing, only bowing his head a little. For some moments they sat in silence. From the village came the sound of quiet chatter and the crackle of flames from a fire. The smoke drifted out from the hut, and settled in an oily cloud over the red-mud earth.

'Maybe I was wrong,' Ngunzi said quietly. 'Since the whites have come to this region there has been nothing but hardship. They have taken our children – your bride. How long will it be before they come for more?'

The old man looked up and searched Tafara's eyes. Ngunzi's eyes were liquid and a sheen had begun to film them, turning them milky blue. Where once Tafara remembered them as being piercing and intense, now they seemed gentle and more and more often, lost, he thought, as though the world was changing around him and he no longer knew which way to turn. Ngunzi seemed more unsteady on his feet and often stumbled as he walked.

'We should send out another messenger,' Tafara said. 'Take a goat, or one of the head of cattle, though we have few enough left as it is.'

Ngunzi nodded. In the hard earth he drew a shape with his

long fingernail. 'Have you heard of the rebellion?'

'There have been some attacks on the villages of the whites. A farm burned here and there. The families flee back to their main stockade and then they send out their warriors.'

'Perhaps you were right,' Ngunzi said. 'If Nehanda is calling for us to take up arms against them…'

'Let us see what we can do to find Mhuru and Anokosha,' Tafara said.

He straightened up and looked over to the hut where his friend had lived. Following his trip to see Nehanda he had been fired up to fight the white invaders, but the intensity of his feelings had cooled since he had got home. He was not afraid of fighting, but he was not a warrior at heart, not like his father had been. The image of the man lying in the path with that clean fresh bullet hole in his back haunted him and as much as he would have liked to have believed that the bullets would turn to water as Nehanda had said, he knew that was wishful thinking.

When he slept that night the spirit of Anokosha visited him. He was lying on his back and suddenly she was there beside him. She reached out, her small hand snaking across his skin, arousing him.

'Anokosha,' he breathed, turning on his side.

She lifted herself up and lowered herself on top of him, easing herself onto him. The thin, blue light shone across her body – seemed, almost, to shine from her. Her breasts rose and fell above him, larger than he recalled. Her belly too, seemed rounder, fuller, like a fruit swelling on a tree. The ecstasy that arose in him was so mixed with sadness that he felt like crying.

'Tell me,' he said, 'where have you been? Where have they taken you? Tell me so that I can find you.' And then, 'How is Mhuru? Let me take a message to his father.'

Anokosha smiled, her thick, sensual lips stretching wide,

but she said nothing. For some time he lay with his hand upon her belly and then he was lost in sleep.

They selected one of the finest head of cattle from the herd and checked it over carefully, separating it and keeping it confined to an enclosure in the village so that it could not be contaminated. On the morning of the seventh day they rose early, before the sun had risen, and took fresh, frothing beer in an earthenware pot and carried it out of the village and up to the cave in the hills.

When the sun rose, they knelt in the shallow hollow beneath the lip of the cave and began the drumming. As the mist rose their voices echoed from the granite stones, muffled and plaintive. Ngunzi stepped forward, swaying to the rhythm of the drums and poured the beer on the earth. It pooled, forming spume upon the ground.

Later, Mbudzi led the cow out from the village, along the path that led to the white settlement. They stood on the edge of the village and watched him go, Mhuru's mother crying and calling after him to be persuasive, to find her son and bring him home.

It was four days later when the white men returned to the village, scattering the children who had been playing in the dirt. Mbudzi walked at the head of the small column, behind him were the white South African Police in their khaki uniforms on horseback and the inevitable translator loping along behind, inane grin on his broad face. Mbudzi's head was bowed. He approached Ngunzi first; Tafara joined them.

'They slaughtered the cow immediately,' he breathed, before the translator came into earshot. 'They were furious. Had I not heard the edict? Was I deliberately trying to infect their animals?'

He wiped the sweat from his face. His clothes were dirty and his feet and legs were caked with mud. Tafara could see from his eyes that he was exhausted.

The white men got down from their horses and gathered around. They formed a circle on the floor outside Ngunzi's hut, the policemen squatting uncomfortably as though they were about to jump up at any moment. Their rifles were cradled on their laps and Tafara looked at them warily.

'The edict has gone out that your cattle should be slaughtered.'

The white man flourished a piece of paper covered in dark characters and poked at it with a stubby forefinger. 'Animal Diseases Act number 2, 1881, and Government notice number 53, 1886, require that any cattle infected with rinderpest should be reported immediately and that the herd should be destroyed to prevent the spread of the disease.'

Ngunzi looked from one to another of the white men, bewildered, his cloudy eyes seeing little but pale blotches against the verdant green of the valley. The policeman cleared his throat. He was a large man, with a shock of fair hair and a thick moustache that fell down on either side of his mouth giving him a dour, unhappy look. He took off his cap and ran his fingers through his hair, then replaced the cap again, neatly.

'The cow was not infected,' Tafara said, his voice sounding like a small, hard pebble.

'It was infected,' the policeman shot back, after listening to the translation.

Tafara glanced at Mbudzi who sat silently a little way to his right. Mbudzi hung his head and avoided his gaze.

'We have come to slaughter the herd,' the policeman explained. 'You will be compensated of course.'

It took the interpreter a moment to think of how to translate this last comment, and for a while he hummed and coughed and cleared his throat, until finally, he relayed the sentence with the English word intact.

'What does this mean?' Tafara questioned.

The translator looked at him with haughty disdain. Tafara tried to assess what tribe he was from.

'No,' Tafara said, his eyes boring into those of the translator.

The translator smiled and passed on his comment to the policeman.

'You don't have a choice,' the policeman fired back.

'If you touch our cattle, I will kill you,' Tafara said.

The policeman smiled; a thin, tight smile without an ounce of humanity. He lifted the rifle from his lap.

'I could shoot you just for having made such a comment, you savage scum.'

Again the translator struggled for an accurate translation of this phrase, but improvised the threat adding insults of his own. Tafara glanced around. There was Mbudzi to his right and a couple of the other young men to his left, but there was nowhere near enough strength to take on the white men with their guns.

The policeman pulled out a wad of bundled papers, small, coloured rectangles with pictures and shapes on them. He counted a number of them off and flung them on the floor before Ngunzi and Tafara.

'The money there is probably worth more than all of your stock,' he said, 'even when they were healthy.'

Tafara gazed, bewildered, at the coloured papers that scattered across the earth caught by a gust of wind. The translator jumped forward and gathered them together carefully.

'You can trade them for many good things,' he told Tafara. 'For food and livestock.'

He pushed the notes into Tafara's hands.

The policeman stood up and addressed the others. A short, stocky man with red hair nodded and grinned at Tafara.

'You are to stay here,' the translator told Tafara. 'If you resist in any way you will be shot.'

Helplessly, Tafara stood at the edge of the farm and watched as the group made their way down the rise to the fields where their herd of cattle were pastured. Behind him the red haired policeman lit a cigarette. He clapped Tafara on the back and offered him one.

For some time there was little noise beyond the sound of the women in the huts and children talking in low, frightened voices. Tafara stood silent, his mind in turmoil. The sun had passed its zenith and had begun to slip down towards the edge of the valley.

The sound of the sharp retort of rifle fire echoed from the granite rocks behind the village; birds rose into the air and for a few short moments there was a cacophony of noise. Behind Tafara, the policeman threw his cigarette butt onto the earth and ground it beneath his heel. He pulled back the indicator leaver of his Martini-Henry rifle and idly turned the barrel and levelled it at Tafara's chest. Tafara turned away from the man. He gazed down across the trees and bush and pictured in his mind's eye the rolling hills and grassland where his cattle roamed.

Tafara was not a violent man; he was a hunter, but he had never killed a man. Stooping down, he picked up a stone, the size of the palm of his hand, smooth and heavy. He weighed it. Considered it. The noise of the guns rose in waves crashing against his ears. Above the trees the pale clouds of smoke gathered ominously.

He jumped when the white man clapped a hand on his shoulder. The man spoke. Though he did not understand a word, the voice was soft and he noted the look in his blue eyes. For one moment he weighed the stone, then, with as much force as he could muster, he threw up his hand and smacked the stone hard against the temple of the white man.

The policeman dropped in an untidy heap upon the earth.

Another volley of shots startled the late afternoon. The birds hung above the trees, high up, circling angrily. The air was still and the village was motionless. Tafara stood above the policeman, looking down at the crumpled body, watching as the blood seeped out, pooling on the earth, soaking in slowly, almost immediately gathering flies.

A figure emerged from the darkness of one of the huts, uttered a strangled moan and then disappeared again. Reaching down, Tafara picked up the gun. Hands trembling, he fumbled with the belt of bullets the policeman wore, tearing it off him and clumsily wrapping it around his own waist.

Straightening up, he glanced back down the incline through the trees to the plain below from where the sound of gunfire still arose, more sporadic now, occasional shots. For one moment longer he hesitated and then he moved, not turning back to the huts, but moving up towards the granite escarpment behind the village, clambering over the rocks, moving swiftly, rifle in hand.

He continued without resting even after darkness had fallen. Normally he would not have travelled at night, certainly not away from the main tracks, but he knew the white men would hunt him and on his own he stood no chance against them. The night was dark. The moon was hidden behind the thick layer of cloud. It was a warm night though and he made good progress across the hills, circling slowly back around towards Nehanda's village.

At the top of a high hill that commanded a good view of the whole area he paused to catch his breath and turned and gazed back across the shadowy, rolling highlands. Far in the distance the darkness was broken by the flickering glimmer of a large fire. He breathed in deeply, gathering himself, then turned and continued on towards Nehanda.

9

Thin clouds skimmed the horizon as Natalie reached the village. The rains were due. The previous few years had been difficult in Zimbabwe; the rains had failed and drought had devastated the crop yields. The heat was almost unbearable. Perspiration ran down the cleft of her spine and she could smell the sharp, semi-sweet scent of her body despite having showered and put on new clothes just before she had come out.

'Madness,' she muttered to herself.

The rough track looked down on a cluster of small huts. The ground was hard beaten and thin smoke curled up from the dwellings into the heavy sky. She had wondered whether she would feel regret when she awoke that morning. All the previous day she had fought with herself. There were seats on the plane to England; she could have been on her way back home. But the image of the young girl's face troubled her. The rapidly ingested disappointment, as though she was used to it. And she was flattered, she couldn't deny that. She was capable of offering hope to somebody. She had it in her power to offer somebody something they wanted.

In England it had been different. There she had faced classes of resentful learners; sour-faced adolescents corralled reluctantly into classrooms where they laughed and joked and lay their heads upon the tables, wrote on the walls, kicked each other, prised keys from the computer keyboards. Did anything but listen to her.

Moses was seated beneath the tree in the centre of the village as though he had not moved since the previous visit. When Natalie approached, he glanced up. He did not seem surprised to see her. He did not rise or speak. The village was quiet. From somewhere came the sound of chickens and the constant dull throb of the cicadas.

Natalie felt suddenly embarrassed before the old man. She gazed at him for some moments unsure how to start. Moses' hair was grey and the thin straggle of whiskers on his chin, almost white.

'The school has no teacher,' she began.

The old man watched her silently.

'Memories... The girl... ' She pointed at one of the village huts fatuously. 'She came to see me. She said she wanted a teacher.'

Still the man said nothing.

'So I've come.'

Moses shifted from his seat, rising slowly. His gaze shifted away from Natalie and he turned and wandered across the packed earth. Natalie watched him go, feeling foolish.

It was only as she began to turn that Natalie noticed the figure standing in the doorway of one of the huts. Memories stepped forward into the sunlight and looked at her gravely, hands folded before her. She was wearing the same tattered T-shirt and skirt, the pocket hanging limply.

'You said you were going to England.'

'I changed my mind.' Natalie smiled.

Memories did not smile. She continued to regard Natalie, her face a mask.

'So you will teach me?'

Natalie nodded. 'We'll see what we can do.'

The first lesson took place beneath the Msasa tree. It was a large, old tree and the branches spread for some metres casting a cooling pool of shade. Taking the rickety chair

Moses had been seated on, Natalie moved it beneath the tree. Memories sat on a log, the same one she had been perched on when she schooled the other children from the village on Natalie's previous visit.

Memories was an able student. That first session, which lasted a couple of hours, they talked about what she had studied with the teacher who had been arrested. Natalie had brought with her a notebook, which she used as a journal, and, tearing off some pages, wrote a few lines for Memories to read, which she did with little difficulty. When she wrote, Memories' handwriting was beautiful, ornately curved letters that trickled delicately across the page making Natalie feel ashamed of her own clumsy, messy hand.

Later Memories took her down to what had been the school building. It was two miles south of the village at the bottom of the hills, a small concrete building, beginning already to crumble away into the greedy brush. The corrugated tin had been stripped from the roof. Inside weeds sprouted, standing almost as tall as Memories. The blackboard had fallen from the wall and lay broken on the floor, the traces of past lessons washed away.

The next day Natalie returned to the village and they took up position beneath the Msasa tree. This time she had come better prepared, with a copy of *Voyage in the Dark* by Jean Rhys, a book she had picked up from her aunt's shelf. It was a bit of a dark book for a twelve-year-old girl, but the writing style was simple, and she thought Memories might appreciate the young female protagonist more than the action thrillers she had brought herself. She had also brought a large pad of paper and a couple of biros, one of which she gave to the girl.

When Natalie appeared on the third day, she found there was another young girl sitting waiting with Memories. She was a little taller and wore a grey shapeless dress that had perhaps once been a school uniform. Memories introduced her as Clara, explaining that they had been friends at the school. A little later a boy joined them, Energy, a thick-set young man. Natalie found it difficult to estimate his age. He could have been anything from thirteen to twenty. He was very quiet and nervous and loitered for a long time at the edge of the fields some twenty feet from the Msasa tree. It was a few days before Natalie was able to encourage him beneath the cool spread of the large branches where the new school met.

Natalie was amazed at the seriousness with which her students worked. Each of the children had responsibilities and work to do for their families, water to carry, farm work, cooking and cleaning and caring for younger children; their lives seemed more grown up than her own. But each day they were waiting for her when she arrived at the village, and the clay earth had been swept neatly and the chair and log arranged. Energy had clambered down to the old school and brought back with him – Natalie could only wonder how, considering its weight – the larger half of the school blackboard.

She taught them English and history. The English she was confident with, but without a textbook she felt a little lost with the history. Their enthusiasm was, though, infectious, and the two hours she set aside for the lesson flashed by.

Often the other children would gather around the edge of the tree to watch and listen. They would not intrude and treated the whole thing with a seriousness that at first made Natalie laugh and then made her nervous. Whenever she visited the village she took some time to see the baby that she had found. They had called the child Happiness. He had begun to flesh out and his eyes were brighter, more lively. One of the women would give him to Natalie and then they would all stand around and laugh as she held the baby gingerly in her arms.

The soft weight of the boy tugged at her. When he lifted his hand to touch Natalie's face, she felt her heart flutter. The fingers softly grazed her skin. The baby's eyes opened wider and he smiled, small blue bubbles breaking on his lips. It was so beautiful that she found it painful. Her eyes filled with tears and she had to pass the baby back, and pretend to have a fit of coughing, to hide her emotion.

Memories gazed at her coolly, her steady, serious gaze unpicking her.

'I'll see you tomorrow,' she said.

'I'll walk with you,' Memories told her.

Her uncle had loaned Natalie a 100cc Kawasaki to get to the village. She rode it up to the top of the dirt lane and then left it there as the track became too rough after that point and walked the last few hundred metres.

'Are you married?' Memories asked as they walked up towards the brow of the rise.

'Married?' Natalie shook her head and smiled. 'No.'

'Why not?'

Natalie liked this serious young student. Though she was only twelve she behaved more like a young woman. She rarely saw Memories laugh; not that she was unhappy, but she always seemed to bring her emotions under control. She had a sharp tongue with the other children and was tough in her discipline of them.

For a moment Natalie thought of Lawrence. She thought about telling Memories about him; about all that she had hoped for, all that she had dreamed of. She thought of the weight of the baby in her arms and the old pain welled up and for a moment threatened to overtake her. She paused on the path and Memories paused beside her watching her. She sighed.

'It just never happened,' she said.

'But you have been in love?' Memories pressed her.

They had reached the top of the rise and Natalie swung her leg over the saddle of the Kawasaki and pushed the books inside her shirt, tucking it into her jeans so that they did not fall out on the journey home. The clouds had built up into a dark mass, heavy and threatening.

'I was going to get married,' she told Memories. 'The

wedding was arranged and everything.'

'So what happened?'

Natalie sat on the bike, kicking the stand away, but not starting up the small engine. Instinctively she shrank back from the memory of that time. Of the darkness that had enfolded her. Beside her Memories stood waiting. She wore the same skirt. It was the only one she had, Natalie presumed.

'I changed my mind.'

'Was he angry with you?'

Natalie shrugged and smiled sadly. 'It was complicated.'

The rains came that afternoon. Not a gentle shower. Not even heavy rain like Natalie had seen in England. The sky darkened as the clouds rolled across and when she looked up from her book towards the tail end of the afternoon, it could have been evening. She considered switching on the light as it had become too dark to read, but instead lay down the book and wandered over to the window that looked down across the grass towards the trees and the boundary of the farm.

A sudden rush of wind and the first drops of rain exploded on the concrete patio area at the back of the cottage and a few moments later the water dragged across the farm in heavy sheets. The hills disappeared and the trees were reduced to ghostly presences, barely visible. Above the roar of rain came the deep rumble of thunder. Momentarily the farm was illuminated by the sudden brilliance of a jagged lightening flash. Almost immediately the sky cracked open. The cottage shuddered. The alarm on her uncle's car wailed in the darkness.

For half an hour the storm lumbered on. Water gushed from the guttering, hissed across the grass; wind buffeted the windows and whipped at the trees, pulling away branches. The crack and rumble of thunder became a continuous roll of sound.

And then, as quickly as it had started, it stopped. The clouds lifted. The sun was just setting, and the sky was blood red. The clouds mauve. As the light faded quickly, the darkness was illuminated by the green of fireflies, down beyond the trees where a small ravine ran fast with rainwater.

'Did you enjoy the storm?' Kristine smiled over dinner.

'Zimbabwe is a lightening magnet,' Roy said. 'There are different theories as to why. It has the largest number of lightening related fatalities in the world. I've heard that it's the granite. The radioactivity discharges gamma rays up into the cloud, ionising the air molecules. In the villages, though, they'll tell you it's the *n'angers*, witch doctors, using their power to kill. Back in the seventies twenty-odd people were killed in one strike, as they sheltered in a hut. Mostly, though its children caught out in the storms, sheltering under trees.'

The next day another storm rolled over, obliterating the landscape. Natalie sat in her cottage and gazed out of the window across the back of the farm. She missed being able to go down to the village. She tried to imagine being in one of the small village huts as the rain pounded down on the grass roof. She found she couldn't. Memories' questions had unsettled her. She found her mind drifting back to Lawrence and to the whole mess she had fled. Being cooped up inside the small cottage didn't help. She was glad when the weather improved, and she was able to ride the Kawasaki back down the road to the village.

When she got there, she found it in a state of disrepair. The rain had damaged the roofs of the buildings and caused mud to slide down from the track. Rather than teaching her small class she found herself riding back to the farm to fetch a shovel. She spent the rest of the day shovelling mud from the ground between the huts and helping to repair the roofs. In the evening she sat in the hut and shared supper, *sadza*, a sticky maize porridge, enlivened with a thin soup of *muriwo*, spinach leaves with tomato. Around her the women chatted in Shona, and in the corner Moses sat, on his own, hunched over his meal, gazing out through the doorway at the village.

Natalie tried to engage Moses in conversation, but the old man avoided her and answered only in monosyllables if spoken to directly. The women were not so reticent and once they were accustomed to her threw out comments and questions they demanded Memories interpret. How did she like their cooking? They laughed. Why wasn't she married? Why was she wasting her time coming to the village? Memories translated the questions unabashed.

The baby was growing. Often Memories would have him tied to her back in a traditional sling and the baby would lie quietly for the whole period of the lesson. After the storm one of the women dropped the baby on Natalie's knee and pointed at her.

'It's your child,' Memories translated. 'You should take care of him.'

The women laughed, slapping their knees and doubling up.

'She looks just like her mother,' Memories translated from another of the women. Again they fell about laughing and slapping their thighs. Memories took the child from her and dandled it and kissed it, making the baby smile and gurgle. Natalie felt her heart contract with unexpected emotion.

Moses stood up and left.

10

The number of young men in Nehanda's village had doubled since Tafara's previous visit. Everywhere they squatted in small circles, talking earnestly, conspiratorially, around small fires, *assegais* in their hands. The air was heavy with wood smoke. From somewhere came the music of the *mbira*, a fine thread of sound, constantly evolving, interweaving its melodies, building rhythmic patterns, sounding from a distance rather like water dripping into a pool deep within the forest.

Wending through the groups of young warriors, Tafara made his way towards the music. The musicians were squatted outside a hut towards the top of the village, not far from the path that wound up the hill towards Nehanda's cave. A fire was burning and the sweet smell of roasted meat caused saliva to fill Tafara's mouth. He realised, suddenly, how hungry he was, and how long it had been since he had last eaten.

A gazelle had been butchered and roasted. A young boy approached Tafara with some of the meat and greeted him; '*Hondo*.' Warrior. Tafara took the meat. The musicians looked up and nodded. Tafara felt the weight of the rifle on his shoulder. He recalled the white man he had killed; yes, he was a warrior, as his father had been. A warmth spread through him. Biting into the meat the sweetness of it almost overwhelmed his senses. He felt its juices oozing down his chin, his fingers sticky with its charred fat.

'Sit with us,' one of the men said, indicating for him to join the group.

'Brother, where did you get the weapon?'

For some moments he could not answer them; his mouth was full of meat, his stomach aching for more, his lips wet with grease. He felt their eyes upon him. The music had stopped and men were wandering in from around the huts. Some, he noted, had followed him up the path.

'They came to our village,' he said, when he could speak. 'They came with papers and guns and said that all of our cattle must be slaughtered. They killed them all. Even the healthy ones that had no disease.'

'And how did you get the weapon?'

Tafara paused. He looked around at the faces, curious and intent.

'I killed one of them,' he said, quietly.

He heard the sharp in-take of breath, but felt the excitement, the suddenly febrile atmosphere, like the air among the granite rocks after a thunderstorm, when everything feels more alive and the hairs on your skin stand on end.

At that moment the *mbira* started up again, picking a sharp percussive rhythm, joined quickly by the soft low throb of fingers on the tautened skin of a drum. The music grew in intensity and one of the young warriors began to sing.

'Here, drink, warrior – *Hondo*,' said one of the men and pushed a cup into his hands filled with frothing beer.

They built up the fire. Darkness had fallen abruptly, and it was cooler. A soft wind blew and there was rain in the air. As the fire grew, so did the crowd of men around it. More musicians joined and soon there was dancing, *assegais* waving in the flickering light. Tafara felt the throb of blood pumping through his veins. He felt alive. Felt strong. For too long he had sat back and done nothing. He had been right to kill the white man; they had killed his cattle. Why did they think they could come to his land and take his cattle?

There was a sudden hush and the dancers fell to the floor, prostrating themselves in the beaten dirt. The *mbira* was silent and the drums ceased. From one of the huts a figure emerged. She moved slowly, regally, and yet there was in the movement of her body a tension and lightness, as though she was a bird of prey about to open her wings and fly.

'*Mbuya* Nehanda!' the warriors cried.

'Our land was open to the strangers,' Nehanda said. Her voice was brittle and angry. Angrier than he had heard on his previous visit. 'We did not attack them; we welcomed them, allowed them to pitch their homes on the land of our forefathers. Mwari, the great Mwari, taught us that this land is His land, and we did not deny them.

'And in return they have fallen upon us. First they brought disease to our cattle, and then they grew greedy and rapacious, and wanted more of our land. Wanted to dig within its belly to steal the gold mined by our ancestors. They killed our livestock. Beat our elders.

'The time has come, my children, the time has come to rise against them.

'Mwari is with you, my children, He will make you strong. Do not fear them. Mwari is with you and they cannot harm you.'

A roar erupted from the gathered men. Tafara prostrated himself in the dirt before the feet of the *Mbuya* Nehanda, and his voice joined in with that of the other warriors.

'We will slaughter the white spirits!'

They rose then, as one, each with a weapon: assegais and rifles, clubs and bows. Tafara found himself at the front of a group of twenty young men; each looked up to him. Some were young, no more than thirteen or fourteen, but there were others, some older than him. He looked around at the men and knew that he could lead them, that they would follow him. He had already killed a white man and on his back he carried a gun.

They ran through the night, making their way south

towards the collection of farms the white settlers had established, spanning out from their main settlement, gradually expanding across the landscape. At one point to the West, they saw flames rising from the roof of a farmhouse and heard in the distance shouting and the crack of gunfire. Silently they moved forward, moving across the plains towards a homestead one of the older men knew.

The settlement was little more than a single farmhouse on the top of a low rise. Its roof was thatched and the ground had been staked out and sectioned off to a distance of around three acres. Cattle were corralled within a fenced area and part of the land had been given over to growing crops. The building itself was curious, being oblong rather than round like the local huts. It was also larger than the huts of the Shona villages. To the side of the main farmhouse were a number of smaller conically roofed, round huts, more like the traditional ones the warriors were familiar with.

As they approached the settlement they heard the barking of dogs. For a moment they paused. Behind the farmhouse rose the moon, large and pale and almost full, casting a thick, buttery light upon the scene.

Knowing that delay would cause his group of warriors to grow nervous, Tafara moved them on quickly. They scaled the fence. Almost immediately the dogs were on them. Fierce brutes, the size of wolves, snarling and baring their teeth and lunging at them. The men cowered back, startled at the sudden ferocity.

Tafara had little experience shooting the white man's gun; he had tried it the previous day, up in the mountains, and the blast of it had knocked him off his feet. Recalling the way he had seen the white men hold the gun, he lifted it now, and with a degree of trepidation pressed hard on the trigger. The blast knocked the barrel of the gun up towards the sky. Around him the warriors fell to their knees. The dogs, too, shrank away. Except for one, which fell to the floor with a whimper.

'You killed it!' one of the men said.

Though startled himself, Tafara hurried the men on. The dogs howled and lunged, but kept a certain distance allowing the warriors to move up the rise to the farmhouse. As they approached, a movement caught Tafara's eye. There was somebody outside the building. He was about to caution the warriors when the first burst of gunfire exploded from behind a low wall to the side of the house. There was a startled yelp to the side of him and, turning as he ran, he saw one of the warriors, a man in his early twenties, with a broad forehead and deep-set eyes, stagger and drop his assegai.

'Fast!' he yelled.

Nehanda *Mbuya*'s words came to him at that moment.

'Mwari will turn their bullets to water, they will not harm you.'

Curiously the words comforted him, gave him strength, despite seeing the warrior fall. Ducking down, he scrambled forward, finding a low ditch deep in shadow, hid from the ghostly light of the moon. A second burst of gunfire shattered the stillness of the night. For a brief moment the brilliance of the explosion illuminated the position of the white men, less than a hundred yards before him to the west of the building. He considered firing back, however he doubted he would hit them and realised he would reveal his own position. Instead he crawled forward on his belly, making as quick progress as he could.

He had advanced about fifty yards, when he heard a shout and a single gunshot. He glanced up and saw in the light of the moon the figure of one of the warriors leaping forward close to the building. Jumping to his feet he ran screaming at the top of his voice. Ahead of him there was shouting, the gunfire again, but this time muffled.

When he leaped the low wall he slipped on the wet earth. Falling heavily, he reached out with his hands to steady himself. Beside him, inert on the cool earth, lay a body. His hands were wet with blood and when he raised them it dripped from his elbows. He wiped them across his face and got to his feet. The sounds had moved around the building. He heard men's voices shouting. Terrified voices and then from further away, the high-pitched scream of a woman.

By the time he had rounded the corner of the farmhouse he was too late. Fire rose from the thatched roof of the house, spreading quickly, like water poured out across the earth. In the flickering light he saw the body of one of the white settlers, the head almost severed, tongue lolling from the mouth as blood pumped out onto the earth. Not more than five feet away lay the body of one of the warriors slumped in the doorway, half blocking it.

He hurdled the body. Inside the building it was difficult to see. Smoke billowed from the roofing, thick and dark. The flames cast a wild, jumping light that made inanimate objects leap. Two more bodies lay strewn across the floor. As he stood, the smoke burning his lungs and making his eyes water, a shadow leapt out at him causing him to scream. The young warrior, no more than fifteen years of age stood grinning before him, his face black with soot and blood. In his hand he held up a severed head – the pale, gold curls entwined between his fingers, long and beautiful. The blue eyes wide, staring. A white woman.

Tafara had never seen a white woman before.

The young warrior dashed past him, out through the doorway and into the night. Tafara turned to go, but could not move his legs. The smoke had grown thicker and it was hard to breathe. His toes squelched in the blood that seeped across the hard-packed earth. The sound of the thatch burning had grown from a crackle to a roar and the heat of the flames scorched his flesh.

He stumbled forward and fell over the bodies. The decapitated corpse of a white woman, her belly rising like a high hill. A kopje. The woman had been heavy with child. He crawled on hands and knees as burning embers rained down upon him. The smoke choked him and his eyes watered so that he was unable to see anything, but could only find his way by touch; the touch of burning flesh, blood soaked earth, the blistering barrel of a rifle.

He lay in the ditch trembling. The night was dark. The moon had been lost behind cloud that had shouldered its way across the sky. Tafara's skin was raw and painful to touch. It was quiet. He lay still, too afraid to move.

11

The drive to Harare from the farm was a picturesque one. Sitting in the back of the Land Rover, jolting, holding tight to the handle of the door as Roy sped over the cracked and pot-holed road, Natalie gazed out at the lush scenery. Roy and Kristine had an appointment at the bank, and Natalie had been glad to hitch a ride with them, partly to get off the farm for a while, but also because she wanted to buy some resources for her students in the village.

On her previous visit some young men from one of the neighbouring villages had hung around until she had finished teaching. As she made her way back to the Kawasaki, they approached her shyly.

'Teacher,' a tall, elegant young man said, stepping forward.

Natalie turned. The young man was a similar age to Natalie. He spoke deferentially and bowed slightly, but his face was enlivened by a bright smile that did not suggest submissiveness.

'Yes?'

'Teacher, we have heard that you are setting up the school here,' the young man said. He smiled again, cheerfully. 'We would like to help. We will help to rebuild the school building, but we have no money to pay. Our children too need to go to school, and at the moment there isn't one around here. The closest now is in Bindura and that is too far and it is already full.'

Natalie was startled. The men stood before her, their expressions hard to read. She shrugged, not quite understanding their meaning.

'I have no money,' she said.

The two men stared at her, a look of confusion shadowing their faces.

'I cannot afford to give you any money,' Natalie explained, theatrically pulling out the pockets of her jeans to show they were empty.

'They don't want your money,' Memories explained. She had sidled up and stood beside Natalie. 'They are offering to help to rebuild the school; they would like for the children of their village to go to the school, but they have no money to pay you as the school teacher.'

Natalie laughed.

'I don't need paying,' she said. 'It would be great, though, if you could help to rebuild the school.'

Memories caught her arm, as she sat on the Kawasaki. 'They should pay,' she said. 'They could pay you something, even if it is only a chicken or some of the crops that they grow.'

'Well, Memories, maybe I'll make you my business manager.'

She left Memories looking thoughtful at the top of the lane, a small smile creeping up one side of her face.

Roy dropped Natalie off on the corner of Jason Moyo Avenue and Second Street. Behind her stood the Meikles Hotel, towering over the Africa Unity Square Gardens. The park was thick with stately jacarandas, startlingly blue. On the other side of it were the Anglican cathedral and the parliament building.

On the corner was Kingston's Bookshop, a government owned store and it was there she headed. Browsing the education section, she found some basic maths textbooks and exercises in English grammar. She also picked up some school jotters and pens and pencils.

'You're taking this seriously,' Roy said, when they picked her up two hours later. 'You need to be careful you know.'

'I'm just teaching some of the children.'

'There's no "just" in Zimbabwe, Natalie,' Kristine said quietly, as the car eased out into the busy traffic. 'Just remember what happened to the last teacher at the school.'

'But they said he was working for the MDC.'

Roy glanced over his shoulder, briefly meeting Natalie's eye. 'They say that about anybody they want to shut up.'

Natalie sat back against the scorching leather seat and gazed out at the city. Exhaust fumes billowed from the ancient cars; stuck in the traffic beside them was a decrepit Mercedes taxi, its windscreen cracked and its body rusted. From it pumped Zimbabwean Jit, a fast-paced, up-beat music with a *mbira* like sound created on the electric guitar. The taxi driver, a worn man of indeterminate age looked up and, catching Natalie's eye, grinned at her and raised his thumb. From below his seat he pulled out a bottle wrapped in brown paper and took a swig and grinned wider.

Natalie felt a sudden chill in the pit of her stomach at Roy's warning. She could not imagine who might have the slightest interest in her teaching some of the children from the village. She was not a politician or even interested in the political situation. It cast a shadow over her mood and as they made their way back to the farm Natalie felt a prick of resentment at her uncle and aunt.

When they arrived back, she excused herself quickly and went to her cottage, shutting the door and throwing the books and pens onto the bed. The maid had cleaned the room, and there was Fanta in the small fridge, cold, with perspiration slipping down the side of glass. She took one out thankfully and, flipping off the cap, took it out to the veranda and sat watching as the sun began its quick descent, listening to the throb of the cicadas and the frogs finding their voice again now that the heat of the day was subsiding.

12

Just before sunrise Tafara thought he heard a noise. Heart thumping, he eased his head up enough to see above the ridge of the hollow in which he hid. He strained his eyes but could see nothing, only the smouldering remains of the house on the top of the hill, sparks picked up occasionally by the gusts of wind, trailing lazily across the black sky. At one point he slept, but dreamt of the white woman's head bobbing bloodily on the end of her blonde hair, and he awoke immediately cold with fright.

As the sky lightened slowly behind the scum of cloud, Tafara moved. Scuttling through the undergrowth, keeping low, alert not only for the sounds of the white warriors come to seek revenge, as inevitably they must, but also for sounds of the other Shona warriors, those of his own raiding party. The idea of meeting them filled him with horror.

At midday he found a stream, up in the ridges of the mountains. Greedily he drank from it and then washed. The dried blood and dirt ran from his body, discolouring the pure flow. He was no warrior, he thought, gazing down through the glittering sheen of water at the pebbles, not seeing the reflection of himself that rippled upon the surface.

Avoiding looking at it.

He longed only for his village, for life as it had been.

For the slow rhythms of his days, the care of the cattle, the sounds of the children and the women singing. Longed for nothing more than to sit outside his hut and watch as the sun descended across the valley. For the companionship of his brothers and the knowledge that Ngunzi could teach him of the ways of the ancestors.

He slept that night in the hollow of a rock in the mountains. Weary from his journey and from the lack of sleep the previous night, he fell asleep almost immediately. At first it was peaceful; for three hours he did not move, but slept like one of the dead, curled in the corner of his refuge. The moon had risen and climbed into the sky when his father appeared. Chimukoko stood above him, his chest bared to the moon – the flesh restored to it, so that he no longer stood stooped, body frail as Tafara recalled him from the last years, but proud, strong as he remembered him being when he was a child.

'Father,' he said.

But his father said nothing, just stood, *assegai* in hand, staring down at him darkly. And when his father was gone, he wept.

Later Anokosha came to him. She ran her fingers across his face, her nails clicked through his hair. When she moved out of the shadow he could see that her breasts were heavier, that her belly had grown. That she was with child. His child. He held his hand against the warm, taut skin of her belly and wondered.

'You are carrying my child,' he said to her.

She smiled and touched him tenderly.

'I will come for you,' he promised, but she turned her face away from him.

'I will come,' he assured her. 'I will bring you back to the village and we will raise our child there.'

She took him in her hand and guided him into her. Gently easing her weight down. She moved slowly and only when he came did he notice that she was silently weeping, hands cradling her distended belly.

He awoke as dawn broke.

He arrived back at his village at the end of the next day, having not met a single person on the journey. The previous evening he had seen a column of white soldiers riding west. There was something sombre and determined about them that cast fear into his heart. He retreated further up into the mountain, keeping as far from their path as possible.

The village was deserted. Many of the huts had been burned to the ground and the ground itself was littered with the shards of broken pottery and clothing. The embers were cold and no smoke rose into the cool air; it had been burned some days before, probably, he thought, the day he had left.

The day that he had killed the white man.

He squatted down in the ruins of his home and wept.

13

Over the next few weeks Natalie's class grew to five. Three girls and two boys all around the same age as Memories apart from one of the boys who was sixteen. Memories was by far the most able of the students; she was attentive and learned quickly. She was an able reader and devoured all of the books Natalie gave her. She did not enjoy mathematics as much, but she learned what she was taught and when Natalie left her with exercises to do, she had always completed them by the next time she came.

On the first Monday of November the school room had been repaired enough to start teaching lessons there. They gathered in the village and walked down to the building together. The children buzzed with excitement. Behind them some of the mothers followed and ahead, proudly, the young men from the neighbouring village led the way.

It was a clear day; the storm clouds that had been building up over the previous days had dissipated and the air was lighter and the sky clear. Outside the school the flame trees were ablaze with colour and the grass, which on her previous visit had been overgrown and neglected, had been cut roughly short.

While one side of the low building remained dilapidated, the main classroom had been cleared and repaired. Sufficient corrugated tin roofing had been salvaged from the rest of the buildings to cover the classroom. The inside had been swept clean, with all undergrowth cleared and the mould scrubbed from the walls; there was no glass in the windows, but there never had been. Five desks and a number of chairs were all that was left of the school furniture and the young men confessed that they had to argue with locals to return those chairs from their village huts.

The students seated themselves, the older ones on the desks and chairs, the younger ones on the floor, while many of the mothers and the young men stood at the back of the room as Natalie began her lesson. She had prepared a lesson on poetry. While she found it difficult pitching a lesson to such a wide variety of ages and abilities, the fact that the students were so keen and so ready to try work, made it easier than teaching in England.

While the younger students happily gathered describing words, she got the older students to work on similes and metaphors. After half an hour she glanced around. The students were all working, heads down, the younger ones sprawled across the floor, struggling with the pencils, the older ones bent low over their new school jotters and she felt a sudden burst of pride as well as fear. It was a school. Twelve students now. She marvelled at how seriously they all took it. The parents who had lingered at the back of the classroom too.

At the end of the lessons that day, she set out a timetable. Each weekday from ten o'clock through to one-thirty she would teach them. If they were going to attend they must come every day and take the lessons seriously. And with Memories prompting, she told them of the cost. Every few weeks they would have to bring her some eggs, or some fruit or some other produce they could afford. Memories warned her that if she did not make them pay they would not take her school seriously.

'What would I do with the eggs and the fruit?' Natalie asked.

Memories looked at her, her wide brow furrowed slightly. 'You would eat them.'

'But we have more than enough food up at the farm.'

Memories shook her head and fell back on her first argument. 'If you do not ask them to pay, they will not take you seriously. That is how it is.'

She loved Memories' serious face and the earnestness of her manner. Nodding then, she agreed. She would, she decided, leave any of the produce she managed to gather at the village.

It was at twelve o'clock a few days later that the police paid a visit. They had just begun a lesson on multiplication and Natalie had summoned Memories to the front of the class to model a simple sum. Memories approached the blackboard seriously and took the broken stick of chalk. She enjoyed being at the front of the class and more and more often Natalie was calling upon her to help with some of the younger children.

As Memories stood at the blackboard writing the figures up with a careful hand in the way she had taught her, Natalie saw the faces of the children turn suddenly and felt the atmosphere of the class change. The students stiffened. Swivelling around, she noticed two figures in the doorway, dark shadows, the brilliant sunshine behind them. It was not until one of them stepped forward that she realised they were policemen.

A sudden silence descended upon the classroom. The whispering, the sound of pencils scratching on paper, even the breathing seemed to cease as the children watched.

As the policeman moved from the doorway he became visible. He wore a pale blue shirt and trousers, which were creased and frayed at the cuffs and the collar. His hair was short and he was clean-shaven. His cap was tucked beneath his arm. He looked around the classroom, as if admiring the work that had been done on it. Bending down he examined the book of one of the younger students, nodding his head slowly. The girl sat silently, frozen.

'Is everything okay?' Natalie said, seeing the fear in the children's faces.

The policeman stood up, stretching. Natalie could not but notice the pistol in its leather holster on his belt. A bead of sweat stood out on the policeman's forehead. He smiled. Natalie had not seen him before; he had not been one of the policemen at the station in Bindura.

'So,' the policeman said, a nod of his head indicating the room as he spoke. 'You've opened the school again.'

'We're just doing some lessons,' Natalie explained.

Memories had stopped writing on the board. She stood with her back to the wall, behind Natalie, staring at the policeman as he advanced across the classroom.

'Carry on,' the policeman told her. 'Let's see what you can do. Let's see what the teacher has been teaching you.'

Memories turned back to the board and continued with the sum. Natalie saw the almost imperceptible quiver of her hand, and the uneven execution of the figures on the board. She wanted to comfort her, to tell her that it was all right, to hug her, but she said nothing and did not move. Memories finished the sum, stood back for a second to reflect on it, made clearer where she had carried a number over from one column to another, then, content, she turned and, handing the chalk to Natalie, went back to sit in her seat.

The policeman clapped slowly and, throwing back his head, laughed. Natalie could not tell if he was being ironic.

For some moments they stood silent, the children staring. No one moved. Then the policemen nodded again and turned away.

'Well, carry on, then,' he said. 'Carry on.'

When he had gone the students giggled nervously.

Natalie finished the lessons early that day. After the students had left, Memories helped her to tidy the classroom. A cupboard had been salvaged from one of the rooms and

Natalie had fixed a lock to it. They kept the books and resources locked safely away. Memories swept the floor with a twig brush and then wiped down the board with a damp cloth.

'I think I should go to the police station,' Natalie said to her.

She perched on a table and Memories came and sat in one of the chairs looking up at her.

'Why?'

'I think I should explain what I have been doing; let them know that I'm not getting paid for it. They may think I'm doing some business here, and I shouldn't be doing that without the correct visas.'

Memories shrugged.

'You think they will close the school down again?' she asked.

Natalie got up and walked across to the window. She gazed out across the parched grass and the stunted trees. A rough gravel parade ground stood off to the left side of the school and on the opposite side of that there were other dilapidated classrooms, their windows empty, vegetation poking through them, like eye-sockets in old skulls.

'I don't know,' she said.

They walked back up to the village in silence, each preoccupied by their thoughts. It was not until they were close to the huts that Natalie noticed Memories had been unusually quiet. Though she was serious, Memories liked to talk and to ask questions; she was endlessly interested in what life was like in England and often quizzed her relentlessly about what her home had been like, what kind of things she owned, how people behaved and especially about school in England.

At first she had answered her flippantly and with irony, but this annoyed Memories and after a while Natalie noted that it was her intense curiosity that drove the questions. She could see the young girl trying to picture the outside world in her head, as though by doing so – by building up that image – she could begin to make a movement out of the limiting restrictions of the village.

'What do you want to do when you are older?' she had asked her once.

Memories pursed her lips and closed her eyes, thinking before she answered.

'I would like to be a teacher,' she said finally. 'I would like to go to college to study and then become a teacher.'

'That's great,' Natalie said. 'You're bright, you could do that.'

She opened her eyes and looked at Natalie. For some moments she said nothing. When she spoke her voice was flat and so mature Natalie felt herself blush.

'I am from a village without a proper school. We have no money. I won't be going to college – that is for white people, and for some people in the city.'

The village was quiet. Moses was seated beneath the Msasa tree gazing out across the fields. The children were nowhere to be seen and the women were in the huts. A couple of emaciated chickens pecked in the dust. At the edge of the village, Natalie took the path up to where she had left the Kawasaki. Memories stood still on the edge of the village and watched her go.

'Natalie,' she called.

Natalie turned. Memories' face was dark and sad. She raised her eyebrows questioningly and then forced a smile.

'It's not so bad,' Natalie said. 'It'll be okay.'

'The baby is sick.' Memories said. She looked down at the floor, her toe scuffing the dust.

'Happiness is sick.'

14

Kare, kare. Long, long ago… We are drawing to the close of my grandfather's story, though he is still so young. He was sixteen that year of the uprising, the first Chimurenga. The people had risen all across Mashonaland, following the example of the Ndebeles. Across the country settlements went up in flames. The white settlers fled back to the forts, the strongholds and the voice of Nehanda was heard across all the land.

Tafara had arrived back at his village late in the day. The light was almost gone and the air heavy with the scent of burnt thatch. There was little left of the buildings: charred pots, broken and scattered across the earth, crumpled walls. On the branch of a tree the remnants of some clothing hung limp and damp, fragile reminders of the family that had lived there. No smoke rose from the remains of the thatch of the huts; the fires had gone out long before. There was no sign of the inhabitants. A lone cockerel sat forlornly on the granite rock behind the village, silent, its head moving jerkily from side to side.

Tafara squatted down in the middle of his home, the scent of the smouldering ruins filling his nostrils. Taking the ashes from the ground, he held them above his head and let them drop down upon him like snow, settling in his hair, on the bridge of his nose, on his shoulders. Handful after handful, until the air was full of powdery dust and he was choking from it and tears ran from his eyes. As his vision blurred he saw again the bodies contorted in the burning kraal, and the blood on his hands, and then the policeman as he collapsed to the floor. And in his mind's eye he saw Ngunzi, Mbudzi, Kamba, his aunts and sisters forced from their homes, from the huts that they had been born in, from the village their family had lived in for generations, and forced to watch as the white men lit the fires.

His mind lingered on Ngunzi, almost blind now, bent double as he walked, his hair as grey as the ash that caked Tafara's body; Ngunzi forced to march at the point of the white man's gun, to leave behind his beloved village, the rocks, the fields, the places where the ancestral spirits dwelled.

In the treetops the birds called their familiar songs, but nothing was familiar anymore. The world had changed. He saw that now. Nehanda's words had meant nothing. The white man's bullets had not turned to water, nor would they. The white man had come and he had changed everything. The white man had no desire to live side-by-side with the Shona, he suddenly realised. It was not a case of sharing the land, they had come to take the land and they would.

That night he slept up on the top of the rocks. He lay out one last time on the granite and gazed up at the heavens, at the vast array of the stars that his father had first shown him; he felt the dense darkness, the warmth of the rock gradually seeping away into the night. He listened to the sounds of the land, the forest, the wind in the rocks, the voices of the spirits, of his ancestors. The voices of the rocks, the trees and the grass, of the bushes and brook, the spirit of the antelope, the hare, the cow, the birds. He listened to a world that he felt in his bones was dying, trying not to fall asleep, trying not to allow himself to miss one moment of it, trying, if he could, to capture it in his soul, that until he died he may retain the memory of it.

When, finally, he did fall asleep he dreamed that he was a baby left out upon the rock. Birds circled in the dark sky, their eyes glittering like the stars. And slowly he realised it was not him at all, but his child, Anokosha's child left out as an offering upon the rock. In his sleep he gazed down at his child, soaring above it with the harrier hawk and the jackal buzzard. Breaking from the thicket he stood above the child, a *duiker*, a leopard, heart thumping, accepting the offering.

The next day, he set out west following the road they had taken Mhuru and Anokosha on.

On a gentle rise, on the southern bank of the Mazowe River, a new settlement was being erected. The uprising did not seem to have affected the work, and as Tafara drew close he saw that a large number of men were working on the buildings. The work was directed by a large Shona, with broad shoulders, dressed in white man's clothes. A number of buildings were being constructed, most on traditional lines, round, with conical thatched roofs, but behind these a larger house was rising, square in shape, built with brick, and a large chimney at its rear. The bricks were being made at the back of the camp, down close to the river. On either side of the Mazowe, figures moved across the fields gathering grass for thatch.

Tafara squatted by the banks of the river and gazed for some time at the work. He noted a single white man, dressed not in khaki, nor like the settlers he had seen on the kraals, but rather in black from head to toe, though there seemed to be a strip of white cloth around his throat. The white man paced the settlement energetically, sometimes speaking to the Shona foreman, sometimes directing the work of the men on the large, brick-built house. Occasionally he himself would pick up some of the materials and show the labourer how he wanted it. The settlement buzzed with energy and the work was coordinated and disciplined in a way Tafara had not witnessed before.

'Brother,' he called out when some of the men walked by, carrying the grass up to the settlement site. 'Who is the white man you are working for?'

'He is a spirit man,' the worker said, using the common Shona term, *N'anga*, for a spirit medium.

'Brother,' Tafara said, as the man turned, the grass piled thick across his shoulder to move up the slope towards the buildings. 'Maybe the N'anga will give me work?'

Work for the white spirit-medium was not hard. Not being skilled in any particular craft, Tafara was set to work in the fields cutting the long grass that would be used as thatch for the cottage. They rose early, before the sun had risen and worked through the day, stopping for a brief period during the full heat of the afternoon.

Any complaints the men might have had about the work were mitigated by the example of the white man himself, who never seemed to flag. He rose earlier than the men and was still awake, sat on a rough wooden stool by a crudely fashioned table writing by the light of a lamp that burned, giving off an acrid foul-smelling smoke. More than once the men speculated around the fire that the white man was inhuman, that he himself was a spirit, a ghost, who had no need of sleep.

If that was the case, then he was a benign one. He showed great concern for the welfare of the men, and even nursed one young boy who suffered from fever. Each day he would wander around the settlement inspecting the work, smiling, a small, worried smile, friendly but seeming as though he bore some invisible weight upon his shoulders.

Each Sunday the men were given the day off, and the white man led prayers in the large building that had almost been completed. Tafara listened to the sound of his sonorous voice, its strange intonation, and the sound of the singing, a curious mixture of Shona song and something different, exotic, full of love for Mwari who had died and come back to life again. Sometimes he longed to go up there and join the men, but he didn't. He lay on his bed of straw and gazed up into the dark shadows and thought of his village, and his mother and sisters, and of old Ngunzi and whether he was still alive. He thought of Anokosha, the bride he had lost and of the child of his dreams. And in his heart he nursed his anger. An impotent, cancerous hatred.

It was about this time that they killed Nehanda. The uprising had been faltering for months as more and more white soldiers marched up from the South where they had already crushed the Ndebele. Word that Nehanda had been taken captive spread quickly across the country and the last hopes of taking back the hills and valleys from the white men faded.

Nehanda was held in the main white settlement of Salisbury. She was charged with having been complicit in the murder of a white Commissioner, named Pollard. The white spirit-medium, Father Bruce, told them of the arrests the following Sunday morning.

All the workers had been summoned to the main building that morning, and the service was held outside under a lowering sky. A blustery wind shook the leaves on the baobab trees and lifted the newly laid thatch on the roofs of the houses.

'Many of those who led the rebellion, have bowed in repentance,' Father Bruce told them, speaking mainly through his interpreter, a thin, intelligent young Shona who had taken on the white name Bernard. 'They have accepted Mwari who the white man calls Jehovah Jesus and the power of his grace.' And then the white man called upon Mwari, raising his hands up towards the dark clouds and declaiming in accented Shona, thanking Him for His grace.

Later that night, as they sat around the fire, a different story was told. '*Mbuya* Nehanda, they could not kill her,' an elderly worker, with grizzled grey hair whispered. 'I know. I have heard it.'

'She is dead,' another said across the flames. 'I have heard it too.'

The elderly man shook his head vehemently. 'No, no,' he muttered, 'you have not heard the story in its full. Yes, they took *Mbuya* Nehanda and others too. And the others, yes, it is true, so they say, that they repented of their deeds and turned to the white man's God, this Jesus Mwari. But Nehanda would not. She stood firm to the end.

'They took them and hung them. Even those that had repented and converted to the white man's religion. They hung them all. But when they tried to hang *Mbuya* Nehanda, they could not. They hung her once, but she did not die. They tried a second time, and still she did not die, because the spirit was in her.

'Before she died, she said to the Catholic priest, 'My bones will rise again.' I heard that he was so incensed that he struck her in the face. The third time they hung her and she died.'

A heavy silence fell upon the men. Above the sound of their breathing came the sound of the crackling of the fire and the wind fluttering the leaves and thrashing the dry grass. Beyond that was the sound of frogs, full throated in the brook at the bottom of the slope and beyond that, faintly, the sound of the white man, Father Bruce, singing.

'My bones will rise again,' the grizzled old man repeated. 'That is what she said.'

Tafara hoarded those words. Nursed them in his bosom. Recited them to himself at night, like a prayer, like the prayer of the white man that he forced them to repeat. 'My bones will rise again.'

Some days after these events a message arrived for Tafara. The messenger was a tall, thin man with a long scar down the left side of his face. When he arrived on the fields of Mazowe he was hungry and tired.

'For many months I have been searching,' he said, pushing

the bread that Tafara had given him into his mouth. 'I did not think that I would find you.'

Tafara nodded slowly. His heart had missed a beat when the man asked for him and was now pounding so heavily that he felt light-headed and as though he would vomit.

'I was with your wife.'

Tafara's eyes darted up and fixed upon the man's face. His eyes could not leave the jagged scar. His breathing came quick and hard.

'At the white man's fort?'

'No.' The messenger shook his head. 'This was on a farm down, far south.' He waved his hand vaguely. 'She had been there some time. When she came they did not know that she was carrying a child. They were angry when they found out.'

Tafara gazed at the man wordless.

'She bore the child,' he continued. 'When I left the farm she made me swear to find you and tell you.'

He had finished the food and looked around as though for more but Tafara had nothing left to give.

'She called him after you,' the messenger said. 'Tafara. Happiness.' He stood up as though a weight had been lifted from his shoulders. 'She wanted you to know this.'

'Where are they?' Tafara said, his hand leaping out and taking the messenger's. 'Where is this farm?'

He looked down at Tafara and his face was suddenly full of sorrow. He shook his head, an action that seemed more like he was trying to free himself from some thought, to shake something out.

'It is no use,' he said.

'Tell me,' Tafara said.

The messenger paused and then ducked his head, his eyes glancing away from Tafara's seeking out the dark corner of the hut.

'They are no longer.'

Tafara stood up. The man held up his hand. 'The baby was weak. They developed a fever.' He shook his head again.

‘That was just before I left.’

For many hours after the man left Tafara sat in the darkness of the hut listening to the sounds of work, the wind in the trees and the cry of the birds. In his mind he pictured the baby on the granite rock. Pictured his bride as she had been in his dreams.

And in his heart the bitterness grew.

15

When the work on the white man's settlement was finished, Tafara made his way once more back towards his village. It had been two years since he had killed the soldier. As he approached the village from the north, from above the precipice of granite, rose a thin pillar of smoke, a dark oily column against the clear blue of the sky, and a feeling of joy lifted from deep within his soul. He felt it rise, painfully, within him. A strange feeling of lightness and suffering. As he hurried forwards, the strength dissolved from his legs, and it was as it sometimes is in a dream when you move with all your might but make no progress.

Though he dared not hope, yet, as he ran, he imagined greeting them. Pictured the family back around the fire: the children, the old women, his friends. He scrambled up the side of the hill, loose shale breaking under his feet, his hands cutting against the sharp grass. At the top of the granite mound, the view stretched out across the shimmering valley, and as he leapt up upon the rock, the cry already forming on his lips and looked down into the folds of the hill from where rose the smoke from the fires, he saw the camp.

The tents were spread at the foot of the hill, on the level ground as it sloped away to the grassland where the cattle had once roamed. Up in the crevices of the slopes were a considerable number of white men. Hard at work were almost naked black labourers. The sound of hammering, of shouts, of metal upon rock, the soft, rhythmic noise of earth being dug, rose up with the dust and the smoke from the fire. Tafara sank to his knees as the bubble burst and his heart deadened.

He found work at the mine and a part of his soul found solace in waking each morning in the familiar setting. The white man had come to extract gold, and had found evidence of a thin seam in the rock. Tafara worked as a general labourer, carrying out from the deepening hole the earth and rock to deposit further down the slope, the work was tedious and back-breaking and the rations poor so that most of the time he felt half starved.

He slept like the dead and worked like an animal and in that way forgot to feel the pain of loss and shut out all thought that life had been another way. That it could have been another way. But as he struggled with some large rock, the granite hardening the skin of his hands so that they were no more sensitive than the bark of the mimosa tree, the weight stretching his muscles, first hardening them and then wearing them away, one thought kept his feet shuffling, his heart alive – *My bones will rise again*.

The vein of gold was thin and poor quality and was soon exhausted and the labourers scattered across the country, moving on to other mines. The white owner of the mine did not move on though. Having surveyed the countryside, and seen that the soil was good, that there was fresh water available and that the granite hills afforded shelter from winds and the rain, he applied to the white authorities and was granted the land to farm.

Reginald Drew, the new landowner, employed a number of the labourers from the mine to work on his land and Tafara managed to secure himself a position. Drew was a tall thin Scot with red hair and a flaming beard. He was a hard man, both on himself and the men that worked for him, never without his leather lash with which he would beat anybody whom he considered to be avoiding work. Many of the labourers left, slipping away in the night, and those who were there in the morning felt the sharp edge of Drew's annoyance at being another hand down.

The first year the crop failed and life was tough. Drew grew even thinner and harder, his blue eyes little more than mean slits in his red face. Twice he fell ill and each time Tafara thought that he would die and that the land would be free again; but Drew was determined not to be beaten and the next year they harvested a good crop.

Other white settlers had begun to move into the valley, and occasionally they would come down to Drew's farm and Tafara would listen to the sound of their laughing and singing until late in the night. When he slept he dreamed of slitting the red haired farmer's throat, but during the day he was a quiet, hard worker, and Drew came to depend upon him and give him more responsibility.

Tafara was almost thirty by the time he got married to a young girl from a village further up the valley. Akudzwe, his bride, was fourteen, a slight girl who rarely spoke. His first son was born the next year; a sickly child that barely lasted the night before its spirit gave up. He buried the child up in the hills with his father, performing the old rites as well as he could. His second child was born a year later, a girl, strong and with her father's quiet sullenness. She was the first of ten to survive; four more died.

My father was born in 1925. Tafara was forty-five by then, and Zindonga was the last of his children. He was born to his third wife, a large woman, happy and careless, who sang all the time. Zindonga was nothing like his father, his eyes were bright and full of hope, and perhaps, because of that, Tafara loved him deeply. Often he would take the boy up into the craggy hills and teach him of the spirits that lived there. They would go to the sacred cave and see the rituals of the old world.

At night they would lay upon the granite kopje and gaze up into the stars, as Tafara had done with his father, and Tafara felt, then, that a thread had been woven between the past and the future; a fragile thread that would keep alive the true spirits of the land that would one day be theirs again.

By the fire, late in the evening, as the women sang, and the wood crackled, Tafara told Zindonga about Nehanda, and about the words that she had spoken when the white man could not kill her. 'Her bones will rise', he told his son. 'Her bones will rise, and in that day, the white men's bullets will turn to water, and we will drive them from the land and it will be ours again. Ours.'

16

'What do you mean, Happiness is sick?'

Natalie stood rooted to the spot, Memories standing before her, running her bare toe in the dirt, cutting a line deeper and deeper.

She could not quite understand the chill that had run down her spine, the sudden fear of loss that had gripped her and made her hand shake as she lifted away the fringe of hair that had fallen in her eyes.

Brushing past Memories, she paced quickly down towards the huts. Her heart was beating fast now. She felt the girl's hand on her arm, trying to hold her back, but she pulled away.

'Natalie, no,' Memories said.

The hut was dark and empty. Natalie pulled open the flap so that the interior was revealed. The beaten clay earth had been mixed with the blood of an ox in the traditional manner, and scrubbed to a high, dark sheen, which reflected back the light that poured in through the doorway. Against the back wall, clay earth-fired pots were stacked one on top of another. In the centre of the hut, the floor dipped and the ashes of a fire gathered in a small grey heap. She let the curtain drop and turned. Memories was stood behind her.

'Where are they?' she asked. 'Where has everybody gone?'

Before Memories had time to reply, Natalie saw a movement at the top of the lane. Stepping past the girl she shaded her eyes and looked up against the falling sun. A figure appeared, a young man, bathed in sweat. Instantly Natalie recognised him and felt her heart jolt for the second time.

'What is it?' she asked, when Bhekinkosi had jogged down the path to the huts. 'Has something happened?'

'*Bhasa* sent me,' the stable boy responded, his breaths jagged. 'He says you must come. The boss says you are needed back at the farm.'

Natalie looked at the young man, his shirt dark with perspiration, and then back at Memories. The girl was watching her, head on one side, eyes large and inscrutable. For a moment Natalie was caught between her desires. She glanced from one to the other.

'*Bhasa* said we must be quick,' Bhekinkosi said, apologetically.

Natalie nodded. She set off up the hill towards the Kawasaki, the young man at her heels, panting hard. Only at the top of the rise, where the lane curved out of sight of the village did she turn. Memories stood where she had left her beside the hut, her arms folded across her thin chest following Natalie with her dark eyes. She turned and straddled the bike and indicated for Bhekinkosi to climb on behind her.

At the farm, Roy was beside the Land Rover, a group of the farm workers around him. His face was red and his forehead lined with deep creases. Kristine stood near the doorway shaded from the light of the sun that was sinking fast by the time Natalie pulled in through the gates and climbed off the bike. Roy was holding his rifle.

'Uncle Roy?'

Roy strode over to her. He clapped a hand on her shoulder and attempted a grin, but it came out more like a grimace.

'There has been a raid on one of the neighbouring farms,'

Roy explained. 'The so-called War Veterans have brought their rag-tag mob of local hooligans and Mugabe loyalists. We're going over there to lend him a hand. To keep them off. I wondered if you would come? Boyle has a daughter a bit younger than you, it would be good for her to have some company.'

Though he posed it as a question, the look in his eye seemed to warn Natalie that this was no tourist outing and that her support was needed. Natalie nodded. In the pit of her stomach she felt a dark foreboding. She glanced at Kristine and saw the worry in her eyes, the strain evident in the skin pulled taut across her features. The farm hands were talking in low voices.

Climbing into the front of the Land Rover, Roy pushed open the passenger door and called Natalie to jump in. The farm workers climbed up over the rear door and squatted in the back. Roy nodded his head as he fired up the engine, and glancing down behind the front seat Natalie saw the sporting Mauser she had used to shoot the buck a few weeks before lying beside her uncle's own rifle. Natalie pulled the seat belt tight around her and gripped the edges of her seat.

'We need to get moving,' Roy muttered, slipping the gears into first and pressing down hard on the accelerator so that the wheels spat dust and gravel as they moved off. 'It'll be dark soon.'

Turning east out of the gates, they drove away from Bindura, deeper into the valley. The sun was already setting behind them and the shadow of the Land Rover raced ahead, a long shadow, black against the darkening road. The air rushing through the window was cooling and blew back Natalie's hair from her face, drying the sweat from her brow. Beneath the trees it was already dark. Smoke rose from a fire in a small village squatted by the edge of the road; in a doorway a small boy looked out, naked apart from the ripped shreds of a filthy T-shirt. The boy's eyes were black and empty; his face a mask, his belly distended.

For a moment Natalie's thoughts rested on the baby, Happiness. She pictured the small child in her arms, felt for a second the soft weight of its body. The scent of it after it had been fed and she felt her heart contract painfully. She was about to say something to her uncle, but turning she saw the grim set of his face, his lips tight, his eyes screwed up and the knuckles white around the steering wheel and said nothing.

By the time they drew close to the farm it was dark. Night came suddenly in Zimbabwe; the sun seemed to accelerate as it drew closer to the horizon, and then it was gone. Roy slowed down, and picked up the CB radio. A voice crackled back, resolute, showing little sign of fear.

'They have set up camp around the perimeter of the farm,' the voice told them. 'Come in from the south, take the back track, you should be able to get through.'

'Are they armed?' Roy asked.

'Sticks, metal bars. I haven't seen evidence of anything else.'

Roy pulled off the road onto a dust track and the car bumped its way through the brush, the headlights picking out the strange shapes of the bushes and the gnarled, disfigured trunks of the baobab trees, with their stumpy branches. A figure emerged from the darkness and Roy slammed on his brakes, narrowly avoiding hitting the man. For some moments he stood looking over the bonnet, his eyes blank. He wore a pair of ragged trousers and no shirt. In his hand he held a machete that hung down loose against his leg. Roy revved the engine and the man slouched away into the darkness.

Natalie gripped the sides of her seat.

'Pick up your rifle,' Roy told her, his voice terse and the words clipped.

Natalie reached behind the seat and picked up the Mauser. Her hands shook as she moved the bolt into position and cradled it on her lap. The Land Rover moved forward more slowly now. Natalie stared out into the darkness, trying to discern the shapes that loomed up around them.

The track soon ran by some barbed wire fencing and they followed it for a couple of hundred metres before reaching a gate where Roy pulled up. He radioed through and before long there was movement behind the fence and the gate swung open allowing the Land Rover to pull through.

'They're up in the main house, *bhasa*,' a voice called through the window.

The house stood at the top of a gentle rise. Around it stretched lawns, and closer to the house, a pool with sun beds and chairs arranged around it looking forlorn in the darkness. The house was single storey, with a red tiled roof and a long veranda stretched along the front. Lights burned in the windows and outside a powerful spotlight illuminated the neatly raked gravel that ringed the building. Two more Land Rovers were parked up beside the house and as they approached a small group of white farmers came out through a side door of the house.

When she stepped out of the vehicle, Natalie heard the sound of drums and singing. The sound chilled her to the bone. Seeing the look on her face one of the men nodded.

'You like the sound of the African night?' He laughed hollowly.

Inside the house there were more farmers. The men stood talking, while a woman in her sixties served cups of tea and cold drinks. The woman, who the men called Auntie Hattie, was thin and wiry with grey hair. She was dressed in a cotton blouse and a floral patterned skirt. She showed no sign of fear. Her hand was firm and did not display even a hint of a tremor as she handed out the china cups. The men were tanned and dressed in jeans and work clothes, they spoke in low voices, chatting about their farms and the problems they were having with crops or pieces of machinery.

'So, this is your niece?' Aunt Hattie said, addressing Natalie rather than Roy. 'It's good of you to come, dear. Janet will be down in a moment. Have a drink.'

She pressed a cold Coke bottle into Natalie's hand.

A few moments later a young woman came into the room. Her blonde hair was tied back in a ponytail. She was tanned, slim and beautiful, dressed in tight blue jeans and a casual white cotton blouse. She smiled seeing Natalie and came over to greet her.

'You're Barbara's cousin,' the girl said, smiling. She had lively blue eyes. Though she was at least five years younger than Natalie, the girl had a social confidence that Natalie immediately envied.

'Barbara was in the year above me,' Janet explained, 'but as we're fairly close neighbours and we ride together, we hung out a lot. I've missed her since she started university.'

The night was quiet. The men took it in turns to stand watch and patrol around the house. Late in the evening Natalie went out with Janet. They stood around the back of the house, on the far side of the swimming pool, at the edge of the light that poured from the house and the spotlight that hung from its eves. Janet pulled out a packet of cigarettes.

'You smoke?'

'Occasionally,' Natalie said.

They smoked a cigarette watching the small fires that burned outside the fence a hundred metres away, listening to the sound of the drums and the chanting of the men, a low, haunting sound.

'Has somebody called the police?' Natalie asked.

Janet laughed. 'I imagine it was the police who sent them here in the first place.'

'Why would they do that?'

'Political pressure. The Zanu MP around here wants to get his hands on some farm land.' Janet dropped her cigarette to the floor and stabbed it out with the toe of her boot. 'And besides that, he knows the white farmers support the MDC candidate.'

'Surely the votes of a few white farmers aren't going to make that much of a difference?'

'If the farmers vote MDC, then so are most of the workers

on their farms. The same goes with businesses. It's not that they are forced to, it's just the way they behave; they don't think for themselves. And they know which side their bread is buttered.' She pointed at a group of farm workers who were squatted down outside the barn around a small fire. 'Why do you think they stay here and defend the farm for the white owners?'

Natalie shrugged her shoulders.

'They know if the white owner gets thrown off the farm, they will be too. The farm will fall into ruins and they will have no work. They have a vested interest in keeping my father in charge of this land and the rest of us; without us they would starve.'

The raid on the farm began early the next morning. Shortly after eight o'clock the police finally arrived, a single patrol car that parked up outside the front gates. Two policemen got out and began to talk to the crowd of War Veterans. Patrick Boyle, Janet's father, went down to the gate to speak with them and very quickly an argument broke out.

Standing by the house, Natalie watched as the men began to shout. Boyle threw up his hands and turned as if to make his way back towards the farmhouse, but the crowd of men surged forwards crashing the gate. As Boyle turned stones began to rain down around him. The large metal gate shuddered under the weight of the bodies thrown against it and after a few moments gave way with a whine and a crash.

Boyle turned again and began to run up towards the house. Natalie felt her heart skip a beat and her hands stiffened around the rifle in her hands. Roy held out his hand and pressed the gun down. He nodded with his head, pointing towards the building.

'You should go inside,' he said.

Natalie shook her head. Janet was beside her father and she wasn't going to hide away, no matter how scared she felt.

'Put the rifle away,' Roy said. 'Let's not escalate things.

Keep it out of sight unless it's really needed.'

The crowd of War Veterans spilled across the lawn. Some of them were men in their sixties, old enough to have been veterans of the war of independence. There were others, though, who were younger, men in their twenties who had been born during Mugabe's rule and knew nothing of the government of Ian Smith, of the Rhodesia that had been. The two policemen sidled up behind the crowd.

'Are you not going to stop them?' Boyle shouted.

The policemen shrugged and made their way up to where the farmers were standing before the farmhouse.

'They are trespassing,' Boyle said, his voice was heated and caught slightly as he spoke, whether through nerves or because he was out of breath having hurried back from the advancing crowd it was hard to tell.

'Maybe it is you that are trespassing,' one of the policemen said. He grinned, though there was nothing particularly friendly about his demeanour.

A woman advanced across the grass, middle-aged, in a blue floral print dress, followed by a couple of young men wearing stained brown trousers and open shirts. They walked over to the windows and gazed into the farmhouse.

'What's the problem here?' Roy said, stepping towards them.

'No problem,' the woman responded cheerfully. 'We have come to occupy the property.'

'You've come to occupy it?'

'Yes, yes,' she clapped her hands together, her whole body moving with her words as if she was singing. 'From now onwards, this is ours.'

Roy was about to respond when the sound of shattered glass turned the heads of the white men. For a moment they seemed unresolved. Roy nodded to Boyle. 'Come on,' he muttered.

Black smoke curled up above one of the hedges and the dogs began barking. Natalie stood back against the wall.

Janet came to join her. They stood quietly in the shade of the eves watching the Veterans roam about the farm.

'Do you not get scared?' Natalie asked.

Janet screwed up her face. 'I'm not an idiot,' she said, 'but I don't think there's anything to be scared about at the moment.'

Natalie felt her blouse damp with sweat. The back of her neck prickled. She glanced enviously at the young blonde girl by her side who seemed as cool and beautiful as ever. It was hard to gauge the mood of the veterans; some laughed and sang, while others looked drugged and carried long sticks and the occasional machete.

The sound of the dogs grew more ferocious and shouts echoed from the walls of the courtyard on the other side of a tall hedge; a group of the farm invaders beat a hasty retreat onto the lawn, the dogs, two Dobermans, following, snarling and barking. One of the white farmers whistled for the dogs, but they paid no attention. Janet laughed softly.

'Get them,' she breathed.

'What papers have they got?' Boyle demanded of the policemen, reappearing, his face dark with rage. 'They have set fire to one of my barns. Aren't you supposed to be policemen? There is still the rule of law in Zimbabwe – you'll be held to account.'

The policemen shifted their feet uneasily. They moved back across the grass and Boyle followed them.

'If this land has been appropriated then there should be papers,' he shouted at their retreating backs. 'Have you checked their papers? Who has authorised this?'

The policemen broke into a slow jog, making their way back to their car on the other side of the fence. The engine started and they disappeared, the cloud of dust rising in the still, hot air and hanging in an ominous cloud above the broken gates of the farm.

The veterans had begun to wander around the farm aimlessly, as if not sure what they should be doing next. They kept away from the dogs, which snarled menacingly and kept up a volley of barks. From the courtyard, on the far side of the hedge there was an explosion and flames shot up into the air.

'There goes his gasoline,' one of the farmers remarked.

With the police gone, the atmosphere had begun to change. Roy and Boyle had joined the white farmers by the house and they conferred quietly.

'There doesn't seem to be any one in charge,' Roy said. 'I think we need to make a move, gauge how serious they are.'

'What are you suggesting?'

'Let's turn up the heat a little. See if they respond or not. You three,' he turned and indicated two of the elder farmers. 'Hang back by the house and be ready with the guns if it turns nasty.' He turned to Natalie and Janet. 'Now, perhaps you two should go inside.'

Janet merely nodded vaguely. She and Natalie moved up towards the door of the farmhouse while Roy and Boyle opened the back of one of the Land Rovers and took out their rifles. Roy and Boyle led the other farmers out towards the main group of veterans. The dogs came with them and Boyle grabbed two by their collar, twisting the leather slightly, tightening them so that the dogs strained more, rearing up on their back legs barking.

'You've no right here,' Roy shouted, moving close to one of the veterans. 'Tell your friends to get off the property. It is private land.'

The group of veterans gathered closer. Natalie felt behind her for the rifle that was leant against the wall. The barrel was hot from the sun. She slid it up into her hands and rested in the shadow of the doorway.

The veterans circled, but as soon as one drew close, the dogs lunged at them and they scuttled away quickly. Roy turned his back on the man he had been speaking to and shouted across to Boyle.

'Let the dogs go, we can't be held responsible for what happens if they trespass on private property.'

Boyle made as if to set loose the two Dobermans. The crowd of veterans shouted in alarm, their clubs and machetes raised aloft. A rifle cracked close to Natalie, and she jumped and thought for a moment that it had been she who fired. At the sound of the gunshot, the veterans moved suddenly, turning and running for the fence. Boyle released the dogs, which bounded after the men. For a few moments there was chaos as the veterans raced back to the road and the farmers gave chase. Janet lowered the sporting rifle and grinned.

Back at their own farm, Natalie withdrew to the cottage. She sat on the edge of the bed and suddenly found herself shaking. She could not stop. It had grown dark and she should have got up to turn on the lights but she found she could not move.

Later Kristine knocked at the door softly and came in. She sat beside her on the edge of the bed and put her arm around Natalie's shoulders. Kristine was an attractive woman in her mid-fifties with greying hair neatly clipped back from her face. She looked a lot like her daughter, Barbara. She was quiet and reserved but gentle in her manner, not unlike Natalie's own mother.

'What if they come here?' Natalie said, her voice unsteady.

Kristine had flicked on the light, but the curtains were open and the windows were black with night. For some moments she said nothing.

'They will,' she said finally. 'It's only a matter of time.'

'How can you put up with it?' Natalie said, turning to face her.

Kristine paused again before she answered. Natalie glanced at her. She had a good profile. Her skin was tanned and there were creases around her eyes. She looked tired, not scared.

'It's home, Natalie. This is my home. We have nothing else, nowhere else to go. We have no money beyond what is invested in this land, this farm. I've been here all of my adult life. Barbara was born here. She grew up here. It's where our friends are. This farm is my life. I couldn't imagine living anywhere else.' She stood up and walked across to the window. 'Particularly not back in gloomy England. I don't think I could stand it.'

She gazed out into the darkness, her reflection staring back, pale and hollow. After a few moments she pulled the curtains closed and turned back to Natalie.

'This farm has been in the Drew family for almost a hundred years. It's our land.' She smiled. 'It's our land.'

She sighed and walked over to the door, stroking Natalie's hair absently as she passed, as though she was her own daughter.

'And besides,' she said, half turning at the door. 'I love it here. The bastards are not going to drive me out.'

It was very early the next morning when a timid knock at the door awoke Natalie. She glanced at her watch; it was not yet seven o'clock. She got up and pulled on her jeans, ran a hand through her hair and opened the front door. Memories was on the step, the sunlight slanting through the branches of the flame tree turning her skin copper.

'Memories… ' She smiled. 'What are you doing here so early?'

'He is dead,' she said.

Natalie felt the blood pulse in her ears. A long, slow beat. For a moment, the world seemed to recede as though she was looking through binoculars the wrong way. Memories grew smaller, distant and the sounds of the morning faded and she remembered with vivid clarity the darkness, the feeling of emptiness and loss.

The world came back with a sudden rush of noise in her ears.

'Dead?'

Memories turned her head away, looking out across the valley, across the green pasture land that dropped away beneath Drew's Kopje.

Natalie did not believe it. Could not.

'He died from a fever,' Memories said, her voice uncharacteristically quiet and subdued. 'I am sorry.'

17

I was four years old when Zindonga, my father, died. Zindonga was cursed with good looks. He was a handsome child, doted upon by his mother and his elder sisters, and even though life was difficult in the late twenties and the early thirties, with white hysteria at the 'Black Peril' at its height, he was a happy child, smiling often, with a laugh that was infectious.

I have no photograph of my father. Only the words of my mother and my aunts and that one image in my mind, as I saw him last. That image wiped all the others away, and for that I hate them more – not only did they kill him, but they stole my other memories with that brutal act.

It became clear quite early in his life that Zindonga was intelligent. He mixed easily with the other children, spoke early, and picking up a discarded book left by the white children behind the barn, he quickly began deciphering the shapes, ordering them, fitting them into a system he picked up from odd fragments he over-heard in the house, or noted from the white children's play, from the words they would scratch in the dust.

Tafara watched Zindonga grow with pride. He noticed the boy's quickness, saw his mother's acuity in his bright eyes, saw her humour in his flushed cheeks, but detected his own stubborn anger buried deep down in his son's soul; too deep for the boy to understand or articulate.

The mission of Father Bruce, which Tafara had helped to build, expanded as the years passed, all the way down the valley. A mission school was set up by the Mazowe River, with the energetic Father Bruce doing most of the teaching. Zindonga's mother was an early and devout convert of the Catholic Church and attended Mass every Sunday, taking Zindonga, her youngest boy, with her.

Zindonga loved the Mass: the crude altar, the incense, the singing, so different to the singing in the village. He took great pride in the fact that his father had helped build the church, despite the fact that Tafara never once stepped inside the building.

'The white men took away our young men, they took away our fields and our pastureland, and now they want to take away our gods,' he said.

Zindonga sat at his feet and listened, looking up at his father who had become stooped with age and whose hair had turned grey and whose skin sagged from his face and chest and his upper arms.

'Our gods will always be here,' Zindonga said. 'Our fathers will always walk this land.'

Tafara nodded and laid his hand on his son's shoulder. 'One day,' he said, 'the people will rise up as they did when I was a young man, and they will take back this land.' He looked out from the entrance of their small hut and gazed down across the fields below the kopje that had once belonged to his family, where he had grown up as a child, nourishing the cattle on the rich pastureland. 'It will be ours again,' he promised. He waved his hand. 'This is your inheritance. *Mbuya* Nehanda has sworn it.'

'Yes, Father, it shall be so.'

And still, Zindonga loved the church. Inside the building

small windows let in thin shafts of light. The walls had been built from brick and were thick and even in the hot weather inside the church it was cooler. The incense burnt during Mass mixed with the earthy, pungent scent of the worshipper's bodies. Most of the early congregation was made up of women, but Father Bruce had as his helper not only Bernard, the tall, thin, Shona convert, but a young man from the village, little older than Zindonga. During the Mass the young man helped Father Bruce and Bernard dress, like them, in a black robe. Zindonga envied the young man and dreamed that he, too, could serve at the altar and wear a black robe and have all of the women of the neighbourhood fussing over him.

When he was old enough he began attending the mission school, and with his bright and cheerful personality he quickly became a favourite both of the other children and of the teachers too.

When Father Bruce died, a young Irishman took over the mission. Father O'Leary was a lean, dark-haired man in his late twenties. With his dark cassock, and his pale face hidden beneath the brim of a wide hat whenever he ventured out, he looked a sickly man; but his appearance belied a will of iron and a quick, intelligent sense of humour. Father O'Leary quickly identified Zindonga as one of his brightest and most able students, and took special care with him.

For Zindonga, those days were some of the best of his life. Whenever he was sent out to work in Drew's fields looking after the cattle, he would go with a book tucked beneath his arm, and lie in the long grass, head buried in the text as the cattle lowed and trudged around the ancient fields.

In the evenings he would share with Tafara the things that he had learned at school; about the world and the great sweep of Western history, of the writings of Augustine. He taught his father odd words of Latin, and recited poems: Shakespeare, Virgil, the Bible. Tafara watched him grow with pride.

Occasionally they would go up the kopje, which

overshadowed Drew's farm, to the cave where the spirits were worshipped, and they would pour out a libation for their ancestors. Squatting in the mud, Zindonga felt slightly uncomfortable with these pagan rituals, but as he grew older he rationalised it to himself that really it was no different to the Catholic saints. And he prayed with his father the old prayers and poured out the beer upon the ground. Later they would sit on the granite peak of the hill and gaze up into the night sky and Tafara would tell him the old tales again; of how this valley had been when Tafara had been a child, of the village that had nestled in the shade of the hill, of wise old Ngunzi and of Mhuru and Mbudzi, and of his first bride Anokosha and of how the white men came and took away first their cattle and then their land. And Zindonga learned these lessons too, just as well as the lessons he learned at the mission school, but these lessons he did not repeat; he stored them deep within his soul, feeding the anger that burned there too deep for him to understand.

Tafara died soon after Zindonga's fifteenth birthday. Zindonga wanted to bury him with the ancients in the cave in the hillside, but Drew would not have it, and he was buried in a dismal plot at the mission, down the valley, away from the farm. The land was barren there, scorched hot in the long months of sun and regularly washed away in the rains. Zindonga crouched down by the humble wooden marker and looked across at the dreary view of the growing shanty town, the rubbish that was accumulating, and felt the anger beginning to dislodge deep within him and begin its slow ascent to the surface.

Following the death of his father, a darkness descended upon Zindonga. Often he was consumed by an inexplicable rage that burned so fiercely within him he was fearful he would lash out at those around him. During these moods he would seek solitude up in the caves, or on top of the granite kopje where he would listen to the sound of the wind as it blew across the valley, and up through the crevices of the rocks and caves.

One morning as he had stumbled down from the top of the kopje he heard the whisper of the wind in the tops of the trees and it sounded for a moment like the voices of many people whispering to him. Zindonga stopped and listened. The previous evening a burning fury had driven him from the hut where he lived with his mother. He was filled with a desire to hurt someone, to kill, even. He had run up into the hills and lay that night on the top of the granite boulder and gazed up into the vast array of stars and recalled the stories of his father, Tafara.

The air was alive. It was very early and the sun was about to rise. As he listened, the sky lightened and a few moments later the sun crept up over the line of the horizon. The light changed as if the brush around him was glowing from some internal energy. At that moment, as he watched, the top boulder on the kopje burst into flame, a brilliant, blinding moment of illumination. Within minutes, the three rocks that made up the head of the kopje were consumed with light, glistening brilliantly in the rising sun. Zindonga fell to his knees.

'Father,' he whispered. And then the names of the gods. Not the Christian God he had learned to worship, but those other gods his father had taught him.

Whenever the dark moods descended upon him, Zindonga recalled that moment, and it comforted him, and he turned his back on Jehovah and called on Mwari instead and the spirits of his fathers, his ancestral spirits and upon Nehanda, *Mbuya* Nehanda.

Zindonga's efforts redoubled at school after the death of his father, and Father O'Leary became something of a father figure to him. Often he would stay at the mission, studying late into the evening by the light of a kerosene lamp. Under the guidance of Father O'Leary Zindonga went to Fort Hare University in South Africa.

Established in 1916, Fort Hare was the first university open to black students in Africa. There Zindonga met young men much like himself. They were bright, keenly intelligent and smouldering with anger. It was there that he joined the ANC and there, too, that he met Grace Mpedzisi.

One evening, Zindonga arrived at the hostel, where the international students at Fort Hare were housed, carrying a bottle of whiskey. Grace was one of the company. She was small and thin and beautiful in a natural and understated manner. As the students partied, she stayed aloof, watching but not participating in the drunken discussion. There was a nobility and a purity about her that attracted Zindonga.

It was close to midnight when somebody burst into the room of the student hostel in Fort Hare to say that there was a demonstration outside the Dean's residence. Drunkenly the crowd emptied out of the room unable to resist the lure of a protest.

'You are not going to join them?' Grace asked Zindonga, who was slouched with his back against the wall nursing a glass of scotch against his stomach. Zindonga did not answer.

When he looked at her, Grace shivered involuntarily. Emptying the whiskey into his mouth, Zindonga ran his hand across his lips and stood up and walked over to her.

Grace wanted to say something. Something that would distract him, to engage him in conversation, to discuss the protest they had been on that day, to talk about the war raging across the world, about their homes, about growing up, their hopes and fears for the future. She opened her mouth to speak, but could find no words. She was silent. Like a deer – a *duiker* – quivering at the approach of a lion.

When he touched her, his hand was gentler than she could have expected. His breath was hot against her face. And she surrendered herself to him. It felt like dying, she thought, but beautifully. Every wall she had constructed, the careful monitoring of her body, the constant obedience to the morals of her mother, the nuns, the faith in which she had been raised

– each one of them she discarded with her clothes so that she felt doubly undressed. Totally naked.

I do not care, she thought, as she gave herself to Zindonga. I do not care.

18

When Natalie woke the dream was fresh in her mind. She lay for some time without moving, the light streaming in through the curtains and, from far away, she could hear the sound of an electric saw. She closed her eyes and tried to recapture the images, but it was the feeling that came back to her; the weight of the child in her arms, the baby she had been carrying close against her heart. When she opened her eyes she thought of Happiness: but it had not been him that she held in the dream. It had been her child. She had known that by the way that it had felt in her arms, by the sharpness of the pain that pierced her heart.

She got up and showered and ate a light breakfast, then took the Kawasaki and rode out along the road to the village. At the top of a rise she stopped and pulled the bike off the road and looked down the valley at the farm nestled below the kopje, at the stream, the trees and in the distance Bindura, just visible. The morning haze had burnt away and it was hot now the sun had risen higher. The view was beautiful and she tried to drink it in, to dispel the knot that held her stomach tight. To forget about what had been, what she had left behind.

Memories was sitting outside one of the huts carefully

washing the enamelled metal bowls for eating when Natalie parked the bike at the end of the track and walked down the slope towards the village. Beneath the Msasa tree, Moses was talking, squatted down close to the earth, beside him, on the chair was a tall, thin man with greying hair. Memories looked up and smiled and waved a hand; drops of water caught in the brilliant sunlight that fell in columns between the leaves of the trees.

'How are you doing?' Natalie ambled down to the buildings.

She was about to squat down close to Memories when, with surprising agility, Moses bound over, waving his arms demonstratively. Behind him, the other man rose from his chair and watched.

'No,' Moses said, 'no lessons today. No.'

He pushed Natalie back, and, startled, Natalie stumbled and almost fell. Moses' face creased with annoyance. His lips were open and he breathed heavily. Perspiration ran down his forehead. Memories rose from the doorstep.

'She is busy,' Moses continued, indicating the girl behind him. 'They are busy. They do not have time for playing at school. There are jobs that must be done.'

'But... '

Behind Moses the other man had walked over and stood close. As Natalie glanced over Moses' shoulder she caught the gaze of the tall man and seemed, momentarily, to recognise him. Moses was shaking his head adamantly. Memories did not speak. She looked at Moses and at Natalie, and her lips moved, but she did not say anything. After a minute or two she sat back down and resumed the washing of the dishes, handling each one carefully, keeping her head down.

'Go,' Moses told her. 'There is no time for this playing. Go.'

Natalie moved away. As she walked she looked back. Moses followed her out of the village, wafting his hands as if he was herding a cow. Behind him the tall man followed and again Natalie felt that she knew him, but she could not place where from.

It was only after she had kick-started the Kawasaki, and was negotiating her way up the heavily rutted path towards the road that she remembered where she had seen the tall visitor.

She pulled up at the end of the track and gazed out through the haze of heat, across the metalled road and down the side of the slope across the trees and fields. A startlingly clear image played before her eyes of the evening at Boyle's farm: the crowd of war veterans spilling across the neatly cropped lawn, the sound of dogs barking, the smell of smoke. A small, squat man carrying a large machete, and behind him a thin man, shirt open to the waist, wooden club dangling from his left hand. He had been one of the men who had gone around to the barn just before it was set on fire. She hadn't seen him again after that.

She half turned around on the seat of her bike. What had Moses been doing with one of the War Veterans? The man had shown no sign of having recognised her, but why had Moses been so hostile? She opened the throttle of the Kawasaki and the bike shot forward, grit and stones scattering in her wake.

'You not down at your school today?' Kristine asked as she entered the kitchen.

Roy was seated at the table finishing a large breakfast and the maid was by the sink washing dishes. Natalie sat opposite Roy and accepted the coffee Kristine poured for her.

'I went to the village,' Natalie said, 'but Moses was really hostile. He didn't want me there.'

Roy scraped the last of the egg from his plate and put his knife and fork down. He looked up at Natalie.

'There was somebody with him,' Natalie continued. 'Somebody at the village. A tall guy. I'm sure it was one of the War Veterans that were at Boyle's farm.'

'Really?' Roy said.

'Do you remember the one with the club? He went around

to the barn just before it was burned down.'

Roy's eyes flickered as he thought. He nodded slowly as if picturing the man in his head.

'Don't you think that's odd?'

Roy shrugged. Getting up, he took his plate over to the sink where the maid took it from him. He smiled and thanked her. 'Why odd? Everybody knows everybody around here.'

Natalie noticed the look that passed between Kristine and Roy as he made towards the door.

'I thought it was odd,' Natalie said to Kristine, as Roy went out. 'Moses was really unfriendly. He never has been before. He wouldn't even let me speak to Memories.'

Kristine sighed. 'It's probably nothing,' she said. 'Moses can be an odd man.'

It was early afternoon when Natalie looked up from the desk where she had been writing a letter. She had heard the sound of a car approaching the farm. It pulled off the road and onto the gravel path, and from her window she glimpsed the white, blue and gold of a Zimbabwean police car.

Natalie got up and walked around to the main farmhouse. Outside, standing in the shade of the flame tree, stood two police officers. Bhekinkosi had been sent to fetch Roy. Kristine paced nervously in the hallway of the farm.

'What do they want?' Natalie asked.

'Nothing good,' said Kristine.

When Roy entered it seemed as though a weight had been placed upon his shoulders. He stood in the hallway and looked around.

'Well, here we go,' he said.

'It may not be,' Kristine murmured.

Roy raised his eyebrows.

'Where are they?'

'They're outside. I couldn't face inviting the bastards in.'

Roy turned to Bhekinkosi, who stood in the doorway. 'That's all Bheki. You can go.'

They sat around the table in the kitchen. The two policemen were sweating; dark patches circled their armpits and their foreheads glistened. They placed their caps on the table. Kristine had sent the maid away and poured them an iced lemon drink herself into glasses cooled in the fridge. The policemen drank thirstily. Roy's drink remained untouched.

Natalie recognised one of the policemen; he had interrogated her at the police station. He was large, in his forties and wore glasses that he took off regularly to polish on the tail of his shirt. He pulled out an envelope and pushed it across the table to Roy. On the front of it was the stamp of the Zimbabwean government. Roy did not glance at it, but kept his eye on the two policemen. His gaze was hard with hostility and Natalie worried he might say something that would prompt the two men to arrest him again. Kristine seemed to share this concern. She walked behind him and rested her hands on his shoulders, massaging him gently. Her eyes did not leave the envelope.

For some moments the table was silent. The two policemen watched, expecting Roy to pick up the envelope, and when he did not they seemed a little unsure how to progress. The larger of the two men broke the silence.

'I think you know what this is about.'

Roy shook his head. 'I have no idea.'

The large policeman took off his glasses and wiped them on his shirt. The lenses were thick, and when he took them off, his eyes seemed suddenly small, squeezed between rolls of flesh.

'Under the terms of the 1992 Land Reform Act,' he said, replacing his glasses and squinting across the table at Roy, 'the government has written to inform you that your farm has been designated for acquisition… '

Roy was shaking his head. A thin smile played on his lips. 'No.'

'What do you mean?' The large policeman seemed to be genuinely surprised. His colleague stared sullenly at Roy as if he was tired already of the whole game.

'I'm not giving up the farm, Comrade Gombera. You can come with whatever fancy papers you want. You know they are all illegal and that they won't hold up in court.'

Gombera grinned. He stood up, placing his hands flatly on the table. Leaning over, he reached out and pushed the envelope towards Roy.

'The papers are served. Your notice has been given.'

His colleague also stood up. He seemed about to speak, but Gombera shushed him. They turned, pushing back their chairs and walked out of the kitchen. Nobody moved until they heard the sound of the front door opening and then closing behind them. Kristine seemed to collapse then, as though suddenly the life had drained out of her and she held onto Roy. Roy whispered to her, stroking her hair.

'Hush,' he said. 'Be strong. We knew this would happen. It was only a matter of time. They've had their eyes on this place for years.'

'Roy,' she wailed. 'What will we do?'

There was a pause, an awkward silence. Natalie gazed down at her hands in her lap. From outside came the sound of the engine of the police car turning over. Finally it burst into life and they listened as it drove off down the gravel driveway.

'We'll fight them,' Roy said. 'We won't make it easy.'

19

Grace Mpedzisi was twenty-one when Zindonga met her; tall and thin with a soft voice. The voice was deceptive. Her family had come from the highlands, the temperate, fertile land in northern Zimbabwe. They had been uprooted by the white government and sent to live on a reserve where the soil was poor; it was overcrowded and farming was difficult.

After their first night together it was some days before Zindonga saw Grace again. He was walking through the leafy campus at Fort Hare when he caught sight of her perched on the edge of a bench beside a smartly dressed young man. Zindonga paused, long enough for her to raise her eyes and see him. She smiled and beckoned him over.

'Hello.' She greeted him cheerfully. 'I wondered whether I would see you again.'

Zindonga nodded to her acquaintance, who was regarding him through a pair of heavy-rimmed spectacles. He was wearing a suit, jacket done up, and a tie despite the heat of the day. Zindonga felt a little unnerved by the frankness of his gaze.

'This is Robert,' Grace introduced them.

The young man rose from the bench, picking up a pile of books and pushing his glasses up onto the bridge of his nose.

Zindonga raised his eyebrows once he had gone.

'He will be a great man, you'll see,' Grace said.

'I would like to see you again,' Zindonga said.

She paused, a book in her hands and smiled, and then rose from the bench. The bench was beneath an arbour weighted down by bougainvillea; the colour of the flowers reflected off her skin, giving a rosy glow to her cheeks. She pushed the book into his hands.

'Read it and then we can discuss it.'

Zindonga watched as she walked away, her step light and confident. When she had disappeared from view he turned the book over and read the title. *An Introduction to Marxism*.

Cutting his lectures that day, he devoured the book. He read on until the light faded. As his roommates went to bed, he lit a candle and continued to read deep into the night, his eyes straining at the dense text. When he finished his roommates were sleeping, their snores rising in a steady rhythm. But Zindonga could not sleep. For an hour he tossed about on the hard bunk, then he got up and dressed and let himself out of the hostel.

He was waiting the next morning when she appeared from the women's hostel close to the university building. She glanced up surprised when he approached her. He felt her eyes slide over his rumpled clothes to the book in his hand. Her eyebrows rose in query.

'I read it,' he said simply.

They went to a small café where labourers and truck drivers stopped for a coffee or a beer and settled in a corner. Grace was wearing a light cotton dress. He recalled the feel of her body, the way her legs had wrapped around him, the hunger and abandon in the way that she had given herself to him, and he longed to touch her, but he did not.

'When I was young,' Grace said, 'I loved the home that I was brought up in. It was small.' She glanced around the café, which was little more than a shack. 'Smaller even than this place.' She sighed. 'This place looks like a palace in comparison. But I didn't realise that then. There was a tree at the back of our home, a jacaranda. I think it was perhaps the only tree on the god-forsaken bit of land. I loved it when the petals fell, purple, pink, it was like heaven, all across the roof of the house, across the dry dust of the yard, across the wooden table.'

She looked at Zindonga. He reached out and took her hand, but she pulled it away. She smiled and stroked one of her fingers down his cheek.

'My father worked the land, and when we were old enough we helped. The ground was poor and we grew barely enough to feed ourselves, never mind have enough to sell. We had a cow; she was thin and barren. It was only as I grew older that I realised that we were poor. And it was only then, that I realised that it had not always been that way; that it was not fate, or my father's poor judgements, or lack of work that caused our impoverishment – it was because the whites had taken our land.'

Zindonga was nodding vigorously. As she spoke he thought of his father and of the stories that Tafara had told him, of how the land had been before the whites had come.

'The whites,' Grace was saying, 'make up only three per cent of the population, and yet they control 75 per cent of the economically viable land.' She paused and pushed her coffee cup away. 'Ninety seven per cent of black Rhodesians control only twenty three per cent of overcrowded, unfertile land. Robert told me that.' She lowered her head and looked at her hands, holding the thin fingers out and examining them. 'Robert thinks that we should fight this injustice, that we should not allow them to take away our land, to force us to carry passes so that they can control our movement. To treat us like third class citizens.'

Later they walked out towards the edge of the town. They thumbed a lift on the back of a truck and got out where the bush started and walked up over the hills to where a river ran, pooling in a grove in a cleft between the hills. It was a popular spot for the students, but was deserted that morning in term time. The air was cool beneath the trees, by the side of the water. While they walked Zindonga told Grace about his father, about his stories of the way things had been and about Nehanda.

Zindonga talked about Tafara's first wife, Anokosha, and how the whites had taken her away and of the dreams that Tafara had and then the messenger telling him that he had a child and that they were both dead.

Grace leaned over and took his face between her two slim hands. She kissed him. Nervously, Zindonga reached out and pulled her body closer to him. Their bodies touched and clung. Her slim thighs wound around him. Her breath was sweet. She was lithe and quick and graceful and reminded Zindonga of a gazelle. He remembered seeing one once, as a child, it had been early morning and he had been out with his father. As they walked back towards the farm they startled the gazelle that had been feeding in the bushes. It passed by very close to him, so close that if he had reached out he could have touched its freckled flank. So close that he could smell the sweet, hot scent of it. It was so light on its feet that it seemed, almost to be flying, rather than running.

When he entered her he gasped and she drew him close and sank her teeth into his neck. His fingers clawed at the muscles in her back.

When, later, they were lying side by side, looking out across the water and the dense thicket on the other side of the pool, she turned to him.

'When we have a child, we will call him Happiness.'

Zindonga smiled. He reached out and kissed her and it was decided then, that they would marry.

They moved back to Zimbabwe just in time for the general strike, which paralysed the country in 1948. After working for two years as a teacher in Salisbury, Zindonga took up a job at the mission school back in his home valley.

And that was where I was born: in the valley farmed by my ancestors.

At first Zindonga was welcomed at the mission school. He was an inspirational teacher, who put his whole heart into education. Our family lived in a small hut in the township that had grown around the mission, a basic one-room home, that Grace kept clean and neat. In the evenings guests would be invited around and then there was talk late into the night, often by the light of candles, or even out under the stars, around a small fire roasting nuts on a flat pan.

Occasionally on these evenings there would be singing and dancing, a gramophone was the one item of luxury that Zindonga and Grace owned, along with a small stack of Swing wax discs; Count Basie, Lester Young and Coleman Hawkins. But more often than not the evenings were opportunities for passionate argument about the future of the country, about the newly emerging leaders like Joshua Nkomo, about Communism, Socialism and revolution.

Vaguely I remember those days. I recall wandering through the chairs, the legs, or lying on the one bed in the corner listening to the sounds of the voices as I drifted off to sleep. The sound of my father. Though I can barely remember his face, I can recall now the sound of his voice; authoritative, warm. I loved to listen to the sound of him talking as the night fell and the people gathered.

Now that Reginald Drew's farm was flourishing, and as one of the earliest white settlers in the valley, Drew became active politically. He was elected to the Southern Rhodesian Parliament as a United Party MP. The United Party preached an ideology of partnership with the black majority. Drew did not have much time for the concept of partnership, either with white opponents or black. He ran the valley as his personal fiefdom and took a keen interest in the developing police force and its control of crime.

It wasn't long before the trouble started between Zindonga and Drew.

20

Roy began his counter-attack almost immediately. Going to his office at the side of the house he made some telephone calls and before dark a steady stream of visitors began to arrive at the farm. The Land Rovers and jeeps pulled up off the driveway onto the grass verges and the men gathered in the house. Many of them were farmers, men who Natalie had met at Boyle's farm, but there were black faces too, men Natalie had not been introduced to. She had been hoping that Janet would come, but Boyle told her when he arrived, that she had flown down to Johannesburg to stay with relatives for a few days.

Natalie helped Kristine to ensure that beers were handed out and that important guests were made to feel comfortable.

'That's James Chiripanyanga,' Kristine said, indicating a tall, smartly dressed man. 'He's a provincial judge. And that is Ruben Nyamabi, the MDC candidate for this ward.'

'Listen Roy,' Nyamabi said later, as they gathered around the table, 'this one is coming from the top. It's no secret that General Muchina has had his eye on the farm for a while. This is Mugabe's favour to him for the attacks on MDC members in this area.'

There were nods around the table.

'That doesn't mean there is nothing that cannot or

shouldn't be done,' James Chiripanyanga said. He had a deep, clearly articulated voice and spoke slowly and precisely. 'Are we saying that we agree there is no longer the rule of law in Zimbabwe?'

'I wasn't saying that Roy should give up. Far from it.'

'You need to appeal against the notice of the acquisition,' Chiripanyanga continued, nodding vaguely at Nyamabi. 'They've served the papers on Friday, and that's deliberate, as I'm sure you're aware.' He took a sip of his beer. 'You won't be able to appeal until Monday morning. If I was you, I would be expecting something to happen this weekend.'

The judge leaned back in his chair and wiped his hand slowly across his forehead. The white farmers drank in silence. Nyamabi leaned forward again; his hands shook a little so that he spilled some beer on the table.

'Judge Chiripanyanga is right,' he said. 'The War Veterans will be up here this weekend without a doubt, you're going to need a plan to deal with them.'

Some of the white farmers stayed that night. Roy walked back to the cottage with Natalie and sat in the chair on the veranda nursing a beer in his hands.

'I'll take you into Harare tomorrow, Natalie. We can get you on a flight back to England this weekend.'

Natalie looked at her uncle. His face seemed to have aged in the time she had been there, the tough lined skin looked tired and pale and his eyes were dull and hard.

'I'm staying.'

Roy shook his head. 'Your mother would never forgive me if something happened to you. You came out here for a holiday, for a rest… ' He glanced up at Natalie. 'I spoke to your mother,' he said.

'You did?'

'She said she was worried about you.'

Natalie shrugged. It had been a while since she had spoken to her mother; in fact she had not spoken to her at all since she had broken up with Lawrence. Since it all fell apart. That had been one of the reasons she had left England. She did not want to listen to her mother's quiet, sensible advice. She did not want to listen to sense. There was no sense to be found in the whole dark mess.

'Not about this,' Roy said, sweeping his hand out towards the darkness. 'She was worried about what happened to you.'

Roy eyed her and she wondered how much her mother had said.

'She was concerned that you seemed to be blocking everybody out.'

Natalie turned away from him. She walked over to the desk and sat down. The photograph of Lawrence and herself was stood up against the line of books. She blushed and would have turned it down against the table but she knew her uncle was watching her.

'What's done is done,' she said.

'It's none of my business,' Roy said, his hands rising defensively. 'I don't know what happened and I'm not sure that your mother knows it all either.' His eyes flicked up and lingered for a moment on the photograph. 'But your mother was concerned for you.'

Natalie sighed. Roy stared off into the darkness outside the window. The night was loud with the noise of the cicadas and the frogs; the air was stuffy and heavy. He rolled his beer bottle between the palms of his hands, then lifted it up and drained it and set it down on the table. For a moment Natalie was tempted to tell Roy, to let it all out. To tell him what had happened with Lawrence and to explain about the child. The bubble welled up from her gut and forced its way painfully up into her throat. She turned away and placed the photograph face down on the table.

'It was nothing,' she said, finally, her voice tight. 'I just needed to get away for a while.'

From somewhere down the road someone was shouting. Roy cocked his head, trying to interpret the sounds, but nothing was discernible.

'Well,' he said then, 'we'll take you into Harare in the morning. I promised your mother.'

Natalie sat on the edge of the bed. The light was off and it was dark in the room. The curtains were open but the moon had been obscured by thick cloud that had rolled in as the sun set. The heat prickled her skin. She tried to imagine being back in England. She tried to imagine the cold weather, looking for a teaching job. She tried to imagine, but couldn't. The thought of England summoned up only the image of Lawrence and what was not and that filled her with emptiness.

She pictured Lawrence as she had last seen him, when she had gone to speak to him. It had been a cold night and she was wrapped up in a large coat, a scarf hiding her chin.

'This is not about you,' she had said.

He had gazed back at her, his eyes clear and blue. She would not go into his apartment, but stood on the landing at the top of the stairs as though she wanted to keep the option open to run.

'This is about us, Natalie,' he said. 'Us.'

She could not stand the beseeching look on his face. She could not deal with his sorrow.

She shook her head. 'No, Lawrie. This is about me.'

Natalie slept fitfully, waking every half hour and checking her watch. The noise of the frogs and the cicadas pulsed through her. Towards dawn it grew suddenly quiet, and she fell into a deeper sleep then.

She heard the sound of crying. Pushing through the bush, she climbed up onto a large granite boulder. The sun was just beginning to rise and the air was strangely luminous.

'What is it?' Roy shouted.

She glanced around, knowing that she had climbed up to look for something. And then Lawrence was there, the baby in his arms. He held it up to her and laughed. And it was

Memories' voice that spoke to her.

'It's your son.'

She woke with a start. The sun was up and the temperature in the room was rising. Her throat was parched.

21

'*Kare kare*.' This was how my mother always started whenever she spoke of Zindonga; as though it was a story, a fairy tale. Long, long ago. She nursed my hatred. She fanned the flames from the smouldering embers, ensured that the hatred swelled. And it was she too, that told me of Tafara, of Nehanda, of the days when this land was ours, when our cattle roamed these fields and we worshipped our ancestors who had lived in this valley, among these hills for centuries. She ensured that the stories were passed down; that it was not forgotten to whom this land belonged, and that promise – 'My bones will rise' – was passed down. The land would be ours again.

'*Kare kare*, when you were no more than a child,' my mother intoned as I lay drowsing in the one bed, 'your father began to organise the workers in the mines in the valley.'

The main mine was in Bindura, a growing town at the head of the valley. There Zindonga unionised the workers and began to organise those in other industries too, those building the roads and the railways.

'United we are a force to be reckoned with,' Zindonga told them.

It wasn't just the books that Grace and Robert had given him that convinced him of the need for the workers to unite;

he had seen the general strike in 1948 when they came back to Zimbabwe. He had seen the fear in the white man's eyes when the black workers rose up. Power, Zindonga surmised, lay not in guns or in money and privilege; power was a psychological state, and it was not hard to calculate how many blacks there were to whites, and how dependant the whites were on black labour.

'They are so few,' he told the groups of workers that gathered at the house in the evenings. 'And we are so many. Without us they have nothing. It is we who have the power. It is we who have the strength if only we believe it.'

Father O'Leary, as he grew older, remained a close friend to Zindonga and often would come around to the small house in the evening to talk. Though my mother, Grace, was devoutly Catholic, Zindonga had lost the faith he was brought up in. Occasionally Father O'Leary spoke to him of faith, but more often than not, the two of them spoke about the condition of the workers and of injustices meted out upon the black population.

It was late on a Friday evening when Drew knocked loudly on the door of Father O'Leary's house. He had been at a meeting of the United Party and was on the way back to the farm in his old pick-up truck when he passed the church.

He found O'Leary in the office behind the church. O'Leary received Drew politely, showing him to a threadbare armchair close to the window and asking the maid to bring in tea. Drew was dressed in a black suit and his flaming red hair had been cut short and slicked back darkly. He was beginning to bald, but his thin, wiry frame had lost none of its pugnaciousness.

'Now then, O'Leary,' Drew began before the maid had even shut the door, 'About this young agitator you're employing down at the school.'

Drew's Scottish accent had hardly softened in the years he had been in Africa. He had been brought up a Presbyterian, but attended church now only because it was expected of him and because the wife that he had acquired insisted upon it; the tone he took when he spoke to Father O'Leary showed little trace of respect.

Father O'Leary paused by the window and gazed out across the lawn. He did not respond, but Drew carried on anyway.

'I'm not having it, do you hear O'Leary? Either you control the munt, or sack him. I'm not having him causing trouble round here.'

Father O'Leary flinched at the farm owner's casual racism. He drew himself up tall and tapped his fingers against the window frame. The maid entered the room with a tray of tea and biscuits and placed them down on the low coffee table. She was about to pour, but Father O'Leary smiled and thanked her.

'It's all right, Prudence, you can leave.'

He took his time pouring the tea, making sure his hand was steady. He even managed a smile as he handed the cup to Drew.

'Zindonga has done nothing that would make his position St Xavier's untenable,' he said, settling himself on a wooden, straight-backed chair close to the fireplace.

'Nothing?' Drew's eyebrows shot up, wrinkling his freckled forehead. 'He's a radical, a trouble-causing rabble riser! He's been organising the local workers into unions and encouraging them to strike. To rebel. I'm warning you O'Leary -'

'You have no authority to come warning me, Reginald,' Father O'Leary cut in.

Drew paused, the tea cup not quite at his thin lips. He placed it back in its saucer and put it down on the table. Standing, he towered over Father O'Leary. Looking up, the priest saw the muscled physique, the body hardened by years of labour, saw the stony look in his eyes and knew that Drew was capable of violence and that many a man would have reason to fear him.

'You should know whose side you're on, O'Leary,' Drew spat at him after a few moments. 'These kaffirs or ours. You can't be on both.'

Father O'Leary lifted his cup to his lips and sipped the tea, suppressing the tremor of rage that ran through him.

'I don't appreciate you using that language,' he began finally, but it was too late. Drew placed the tea cup on the mantelpiece with a crash and stormed over to the door. He turned as he opened it and cast a dark glare at the priest. Father O'Leary rose to his feet, but Drew turned from him and strode out of the room, slamming the door behind him.

Father O'Leary summoned Zindonga to his office the following evening. Zindonga was tall and slim, with a handsome physique. He was a popular teacher at the school; the young students looked up to him and he was intelligent and taught with passion. When Zindonga appeared at the door of his office, he welcomed him in with a smile.

'Take a seat,' Father O'Leary said, indicating the chair by the fireplace. For most of the year the fire stood empty. Prudence had swept it clean and put a vase of fresh flowers in the hearth. Father O'Leary liked the fireplace; it reminded him of home and the small hut in rural Ireland where he had been raised.

Zindonga shook his head. Beneath his arm he had a pile of books and a folder bulging with papers. Father O'Leary eyed it. He took his pipe from the mantelpiece and stuffed it carefully and deliberately.

'Reginald Drew was around here last night,' he said finally. He put the pipe in his mouth, clamping it between his teeth while he took out a matchbox and extracted a red-headed match. For a moment he held it; the red head and the flame suddenly reminded him of Drew and he grimaced.

Zindonga nodded slowly.

'He was concerned about your influence on the workers around here.'

The smoke was oily and heavy and the smell of it filled the small room. Zindonga watched the priest passively.

'He wanted me to get rid of you,' Father O'Leary said then, candidly.

'And what did you say?' Zindonga said. Despite himself he felt his heart thud a little harder. He thought of Grace and the child that she was expecting. He wondered how she would react if he lost his job. They would have to move. It would be difficult with her being pregnant; they had little enough money as it was and nothing saved.

'I said that he had no right to ask such things,' Father O'Leary said.

As Zindonga looked at him he noticed suddenly how much the priest had aged. He had begun to stoop a little and his hair was thinning and his skin seemed sallow and hung from him loosely. He had a sudden sharp image of the priest when he was young, not long after he had come to serve at the church. He had taken all of the boys out to the river. He hadn't swum himself, but he remembered the young priest lifting up one of the boys and tossing him into the water. He remembered the laughter and the companionship of those days. Of the belief that the young priest had shown in him as a student.

'Drew doesn't scare me,' Zindonga said. 'I've seen how he can behave, I've seen him beat men with his bare hands when I was a child on his farm, but he doesn't scare me.'

'Never-the-less,' said Father O'Leary, tilting his head, holding his pipe in his left hand as he leaned against the mantelpiece.

But Zindonga wasn't listening to him either. He shuffled the books and papers from under one arm to the other and turned towards the door.

'Was that it?'

Father O'Leary gazed at him for a moment and then nodded.

'Yes, that was it.'

22

Saturday morning. The farm was quiet. Natalie turned on her bed and glanced at her watch, it was half past six. The sun was up and the heat was beginning to rise; she pushed away the thin cotton sheet and turned on her back staring up at the ceiling. It wouldn't be long before the farm began to stir and then Roy would come for her. A quick breakfast and then into the Land Rover and onto the road to Harare. The flight to London left mid-morning. She worked it out in her head. Zimbabwe was two hours ahead of London. A ten hour flight. She would be back in London in time for last orders.

She sat up and walked over to the shower. The water was beautifully cool and she turned it right down until it was almost too cold to bear and she was gasping for breath. When she had towelled herself dry, she went to sit in the chair by the window, drawing the curtains back so she could see down across the lawn towards the trees.

Lawrence would be a telephone call away. How would he respond if she called? What would she say to him? What was there left to say?

She was dressed when she heard the soft knock at her door. She opened it quickly. Roy stood outside, dressed in a khaki shirt and jeans, a worn leather cowboy hat pulled down onto his head, the brim shading his eyes.

'You ready?' Roy said, glancing over her shoulder into the room.

'I'm not going, Roy.'

Roy looked at her. She felt the blue eyes boring into her and her cheeks flushed but she did not look away.

'Let's go inside,' Roy said, indicating for Natalie to step back.

Natalie followed him into the room and closed the door. Roy took off his hat and ran his finger around the inside of it. Then threw it on the bed.

'You know what is likely to happen this weekend?'

Natalie nodded. 'I was at Boyle's farm.'

Roy nodded as if considering this. 'You never can tell how these things are going to pan out,' he said. 'Up at Boyle's it didn't turn out badly the other night, but you should know that it can get ugly, if they decide. There have been plenty of farmers who have ended up with a beating. There are those who have ended worse. We've lost some.'

'Roy,' Natalie said. 'I've got nothing to go back to England for at the moment. I thought about it this morning – being back there tonight in South-East London, down at the pub. Looking for a job on Monday. I can't do it. Not now, not at the moment.'

Roy eyed her, then shook his head.

'We have friends in Harare. We can take you there to stay for a few days. Just till we see how things go. Get through the weekend. See how we can push the lawyers on Monday.'

'Is Kristine going?'

'Kristine's staying,' Roy said slowly. 'This is her home. It would break her up to leave it. Thirty-five years we've been here, after we inherited it from old man Drew. It's a good chunk of your life.'

'I want to stay, Roy.'

Roy placed his hand on her shoulder and pressed it hard.

'I don't know what I'd say to your mother if something went wrong.'

As he was leaving, Natalie called to her uncle.

'Roy, the other day Memories came up here,' she said. 'She told me that the baby, Happiness, had gone. That the baby died.'

Roy stood in the doorway, silhouetted against the bright glare of the early morning sunshine, his hat crushed in his hand. For a moment he was silent, still, then he sighed heavily.

'I hadn't heard that,' he said. 'It happens, Natalie. A fever. It can happen quickly in the villages.' He shook his head and turned, closing the door quietly behind him.

And not just in an African village, she thought desolately. Turning she went to the window and placed her forehead against the glass. One day here, the next gone. Ceasing to exist as quickly as that.

At the breakfast table the mood was artificially light. Kristine laughed and the maid sang softly to herself as she placed the fruit and cereals onto the table. Roy talked about the farm, about the crops and his hopes for the year, of how work needed to be done on the roof of the barn and what a good-for-nothing Bhekinkosi could be sometimes. He told a long anecdote about one of their neighbouring farmers, an old man who was in the early stages of Alzheimer's, but refused to give up working. Nobody said a word about the papers that had been served, or the War Veterans.

After breakfast Natalie followed Roy into the back room where the gun cabinet was kept. Roy unlocked the doors and undid the chain. In silence they cleaned the guns carefully, checked the ammunition, made sure everything was in place and in working order. Only when the guns were replaced in the cabinet did Roy look up at Natalie, his eyebrows raised.

'There's still time to change your mind. It won't take long to get you over to Harare.'

Natalie shook her head.

'I'm staying.'

The heat of the day was intense. Natalie went to work in the barn with Bhekinkosi and several of the other farm hands, cleaning the stables and grooming the horses. She was soon covered in sweat and her T-shirt clung to her damply, but the physical labour helped keep her nerves in check and her mind off what might happen. They broke for lunch and Natalie went back to her room for a shower and in the afternoon lay on her bed writing letters to friends in England. She missed the routine of going down to teach the children in the village.

In the middle of the afternoon a car approached from Bindura and the whole farm seemed to tense its nerves, but it rattled by, kicking up a cloud of dust that hung in the thick air long after it had disappeared around the corner of the hill. Natalie walked around the back of her small cottage and across the neatly cut lawn towards the stream that ran at the edge of the farm. Because of the rains it ran faster than when she had first arrived, licking the muddy edges of its banks. The frogs sounded lazy and defeated, and even there, under the shade of the trees, close to the water the day was almost too oppressive to cope with.

When they ate dinner that evening, a light salad with salmon, nobody said much. The maid served the food in silence and Kristine kept her head down. Roy excused himself quickly after eating saying he had a job on the Land Rover that he wanted to get finished while there was some light left to work with. Natalie sat for some time with Kristine and tried to engage her in conversation, but soon she too returned to her room and sat close to the window reading a book, looking up every few minutes to survey the calm, green lawn. Just as the light began to fade, Kristine sent the maid around to Natalie's cottage and invited her back into the main house.

'I think it's better you sleep in here tonight,' Kristine said. 'I've made up the bed in Barbara's room, you can sleep there.'

It was late when she heard Roy out in the hall. She pulled on a dressing gown and stumbled out to see what was going on. Roy was dressed. Kristine stood in the doorway of their room.

'There's some movement around the perimeter of the farm,' Roy said. 'I'm just going out to see what is going on.'

23

Late one evening in 1954 there was a hurried knock at the door of Zindonga's house in Bindura. It was October and the heat barely eased with the fall of darkness. The land was dry and seemed to call out for the rains. The white settlers called it 'suicide season'. The slightest spark soon burned into a conflagration.

In the late 1940s the white population grew rapidly in Rhodesia; the settlers doubled in number in the space of ten years. Thousands of migrants flew into the country, some from England, others from Eastern Europe, and new housing spread out around the picturesque perimeters of the main towns. The capital, Salisbury, had grown from being little more than an extended village to a bustling town. Bindura, too, saw an influx of new white migrants. To make room for them over one hundred thousand black farmers were moved from their properties, forced onto the already over-crowded reserves.

Hearing the knock, Grace looked up from bed. There was fear in her eyes as though she knew the messenger could only be bringing trouble.

'It's late,' she said. 'Don't answer it.'

Zindonga was sat at the small table preparing some work for his lessons. He glanced over at the door and then at Grace and smiled.

'The light is burning,' he said, indicating the kerosene lamp. 'They can see that somebody is at home.'

The boy who stood in the doorway was young. His clothes were dirty and tattered. The boy could hardly talk and stood stuttering in the doorway. Zindonga knelt down and drew the boy closer to him so that he could whisper into his ear. From across the room Grace could barely hear the child's voice.

I was sleeping by my mother's side, so I too did not hear the message the boy had come to deliver. Nor did I see my father as he stood up and squeezed the boy's shoulder and stepped over to pull his jacket from the hook on the wall. He did not walk over the small room and reach out and stroke my hair. He did not bend down and kiss me.

'Where are you going?' Grace asked.

'I won't be long,' Zindonga said.

Zindonga had bought himself a bicycle and he rushed around to the back of the house to fetch it.

'Grace,' he said, poking his head in the door. 'Give the child something to drink.'

'Where are you going?' Grace asked again.

The boy stood in the doorway looking nervously from Zindonga to Grace. Grace levered herself into a sitting position, and arranged the thin sheet over my sleeping body. Zindonga did not reply. Mounting the bicycle, he pedalled off into the darkness. Getting up from the bed, Grace pulled the boy into the room and sat him on a stool. She dipped a chipped cup into the bucket of water and held it out for him. The boy took it nervously, but drank thirstily.

'I know what happened next,' my mother told me as I grew older, 'only from what I was told by others. I never saw your father alive again.'

Before Zindonga had even arrived at the small farm north of Bindura, he could smell the smoke in the air and see the soft glow of burning. He peddled hard up the rough road, but then had to leave the bicycle as the track deteriorated. As he drew closer the sound of voices drifted with the smoke on the heavy air. The high, mournful ululation of a distraught woman sent shivers down his spine despite the heat of the night.

The light of the fire illuminated the awkward shapes of lorries parked lopsidedly in the grass. Dogs barked and Zindonga saw the silhouettes of figures darting backwards and forwards before the flames.

A man stumbled out of the grass and Zindonga caught him by the arms as he fell. For a moment the figure pulled back, afraid, but recognising Zindonga's face, the farm labourer grabbed hold of him, like a ship-wrecked mariner clinging to a buoy in the storm.

'They have burned the homes, they have destroyed it all,' he wailed.

The farm was a little further down the valley from the kopje Tafara had taken Zindonga to as a child. Drew's farm had expanded over the years, swallowing up the smaller farms on the valley floor, creeping closer towards Bindura.

Disengaging himself, Zindonga marched up the hill to the where the fire was burning on the summit. A white figure approached him, rifle slung carelessly across his arm, a barking dog barely restrained on a leather leash at his side. Seeing Zindonga emerge from the darkness the white farmer bridled, his face tight with hostility.

'What do you want?' he shouted.

Zindonga felt his heart accelerate. He paused a moment to ensure that his voice was in control before he responded.

'What do you think you are doing? You cannot just come onto somebody's property and burn it to the ground.'

He glanced at the flames dancing behind the white figure. They were beginning to die down now. There was a sudden crash as a wall collapsed and sparks rose tower-like into the air, where they pirouetted prettily against the dark canvas of the night sky. The white man laughed.

'They got the letter,' he said.

He came closer to examine Zindonga, and seeing his face, recognised him.

'Hey,' he called across the flickering grass to a group of shadows, 'it's that commie-munt come along to give us a hard time.'

The figures stirred and the murmur of their voices drifted across the dry grass. Zindonga recognised Drew's irritated voice among the others. The crowd moved towards him. Zindonga stood his ground. He glanced around, but the occupants of the farm had fled; only one man remained, wandering dazed and confused at the bottom of the hill.

'What are you doing here, Drew?' Zindonga called.

'It's none of your bloody business!' Drew's voice was sharp.

'You burn down the homes of our farmers and it is my business.' Zindonga drew himself up taller, his feet slightly apart.

Drew came closer and Zindonga noted his furious features in the light from the burning huts. Behind him the white men grouped; Zindonga recognised them as local farmers and a member of the local police force out of uniform. Drew's face was smeared darkly. They smelled of smoke. As they drew closer, Zindonga instinctively placed his hand on his chest; in the inside pocket of his jacket he carried a photograph given to him by Tafara many years before. His father had told him the story of the strange white man and his box and pointed out the figures in the picture, Ngunzi, Mhuru, himself as a young man. And behind him was the village nestled beneath the kopje.

'This is European land,' Drew said.

He stepped closer to Zindonga and he waved some papers in the air, as if fanning himself. His eyes were pale blue, almost grey. 'You know the law,' Drew continued. 'You know the Land Apportionment Act. This land was designated for European farming. This family were served with notices to move to the native reserves months ago.'

'Why should they move, Drew?' Zindonga shot back. 'This is their land. They have farmed it all their lives.'

'Farmed it?' Drew said.

Behind him the white men laughed. It was a hollow and aggressive sound, more like the growling of dogs.

'They barely scratch out enough to feed themselves. They've been allocated land in the reserve. It's the law, Zindonga, and you and all your monkeys have to accept it.'

Zindonga felt the anger growing from deep within him. He looked around the group of men. There were ten of them, all armed, with dogs straining at their leads. He knew then that he should not have come alone, but he felt himself exploding with rage.

'It's *your* law Drew,' he said, barely controlling his voice. 'It's not *our* law.'

'Listen, you little shit.' Drew stepped forward, his red hair burning with all the intensity of the thatch on the African farmhouses. 'This country didn't have any laws before we came here. This shitty country didn't have anything before we came here. Don't you come to me with your stuck up black nose, just because you got an education from some bleeding Irishman. You're filth and you know it, and you should be down on your knees thanking us for coming here to give you a smell of civilisation.'

Zindonga cleared his throat. He coughed deeply, working up a fat globule of mucus and spat it out on Drew's shoe.

'There's my thanks,' he said acidly.

The next morning, early, in the coolest hour, not long after the sun had begun to rise and the earth was still shrouded in mist, Grace was awoken by another knock on the door. This time two women stood on the threshold; poor women, peasant farmers, squat and humble. Seeing the tears on their faces, and hearing the soft moans on their lips, the bowing of their heads, Grace understood their message.

She woke me then, and hushed me as I complained. She pulled a jumper over my head and pulled me from the bed.

'Come,' she said. 'We must say goodbye to your father.'

24

It was just after midnight. Natalie glanced at her watch. She had gone to bed at eleven thinking she would not be able to sleep, but had dropped off fairly quickly. Roy had awoken her from a dream. She stood in the hallway suddenly wide awake. Kristine came out from her room and together they followed Roy down the stairs

The kitchen was in darkness. The night was still. Through the window, faintly, it was possible to hear the faint pulse of the grasshoppers and occasionally the deep-throated, ugly, cry of a frog. Roy's figure was silhouetted against the window.

'Are you going out there?' Kristine said.

On the table was a hand gun. Seeing Natalie glance at it, Roy half smiled at the look on her face.

'It's just for protection,' he grinned. 'You never know. Just to give them a scare. I'm not planning on shooting anyone – I don't fancy spending the rest of my life in the Chikurubi.'

'The Chikurubi?'

'It's a maximum security prison in Harare,' Kristine explained. 'You don't want to end up there. They lock you up, twenty-five to a cell, half of them dying of AIDS or Hepatitis. It's hell on earth.'

The dog, which had been slouched beneath the kitchen

table, got up, its hackles raised and growled. Roy bent down and shushed it, laying his hand firmly on the dog's head, stroking it under the muzzle with the other.

'Something's out there,' Roy said.

'Is it wise to go and see at this time of night?' Kristine's voice was tight with concern.

Roy grinned. 'Why not? Let's see what they're up to.'

The moon had risen a couple of hours before, but a bank of cloud had built up and its wan light was obscured so that the night felt particularly dark. Natalie and Kristine followed Roy to the door, and stood watching as he pushed the hand gun into the back of his jeans and stepped out onto the pathway; the crunch of the soles of his shoes on the gravel sounded explosively loud. He had the dog on a lead, growling softly. Roy walked quickly over to the grass and pressed forward towards the perimeter fencing following the pace set by the dog.

'I'm sorry I haven't had much time for you,' Kristine said.

Natalie glanced at her aunt. Kristine stood leant against the doorjamb, eyes firmly fixed on her husband who was disappearing into the darkness.

'Barbara was always with her father,' Kristine said, and Natalie thought there was a touch of sadness alongside the dry humour in the way she spoke. 'She was always a tomboy. Roy taught her to ride and to shoot. She's a better shot than he is. She won a national tournament.'

Kristine straightened up.

'You want tea?'

Natalie nodded.

'I was never so good as a mother,' Kristine said, turning back into the house.

'Barbara spoke about you often,' Natalie said.

Kristine laughed. 'I'm sure she did. Complaining about the way I try to restrict her. She was desperate to go to England. I didn't want her to go so far.'

They settled at the table in the kitchen. Kristine had filled the kettle and put it on to boil. She had not turned on the lights and they sat in the faint light that fell through the window.

'The truth is,' Kristine continued, 'I didn't want her in England. It's changed so much since I was there. I didn't want her turning out like they are there.' She paused and reached out and touched Natalie. 'No offence meant to you.'

'She loves Africa,' Natalie said. 'It's all she would talk about. She was always telling me that I needed to come.'

The kettle boiled and Kristine got up and made two cups of Earl Grey. She placed the steaming cups on the table and eased herself back down into the chair. She sighed.

'That is the problem for her generation,' she said. 'It's their home. It's everything they know. They love it, and yet they know their future is not here.'

As Roy crossed the lawn, the murmur of low conversation became faintly audible. The dog strained against the lead, but Roy bent down close to it, enfolding his arms around its body, whispering into its ear to calm it. Peering into the darkness he tried to make out the figures beyond the mesh fencing, but nothing was visible.

Roy indicated for the dog to lie down, and it did so, obediently. Roy moved towards the perimeter of the farm. From the window Natalie watched him go. He paused behind the trunk of a Msasa tree, sheltered beneath the heavy branches which hung down towards the floor, their amber-red leaves screening him from the road.

Through the leaves, looking out beyond the fence onto the dust road, Roy could see dark shapes milling. The men were building a fire. A thin flame shuddered in the breeze. They squatted around the faint, flickering light talking in low voices. As Roy watched, more men joined in small groups, looming up out of the darkness and falling in with those crouched around the fire.

The dog was waiting for Roy on the lawn, whining softly. It jumped up seeing him and barked softly. Roy bent down to stroke it. He moved back across the lawn towards the house. Inside, Roy switched on the light. He took the hand gun and went and locked it away in the safe.

'There's not many of them,' Roy said. 'Probably about twenty or so. They're not likely to do anything tonight,' he said, coming back into the kitchen. He poured himself a glass of juice. 'But we should certainly expect something tomorrow.'

'Did you recognise any of them?' Kristine asked.

Roy shook his head. 'No, they didn't look local.' He glanced over at Natalie. 'Often they're not,' he explained. 'Somebody obviously has their eye on the farm and wants us off it. These guys outside will be their men, ZANU men. That's the irony of it all. The locals have no interest in kicking us off the farm, why would they? We give them work, we feed them. When they kick the white farmers off, they give the land to a few of their buddies and they kick all the local labourers off. Often they beat them too.'

'So what will happen to Bhekinkosi if they raid the farm?'

'He'll probably do a runner at the first sign of any trouble and you can't blame him for that. Who wants to get a beating at their hands?'

Back in bed, Natalie lay looking at the light of the moon shining through the gap in the curtains and falling lightly on the bed sheet. She pictured the men gathering outside the fence. She recalled the man they had almost collided with at Boyle's farm, bare-chested, machete dangling from his grip. Perhaps I made a mistake in staying, she thought. For some time, the worry kept her vigilant, her ears pricked for noises. Slowly, though, tiredness overcame her and she slept.

A sudden crash woke her. She sat up sharply. It was still dark and even the light of the moon seemed to have disappeared. The dog was barking loudly. The light on the landing flashed on and the sudden brightness falling through the open doorway hurt her eyes. Roy ran past down the stairs. Natalie sat up, her heart thudding.

25

He hung limply on the tree, his arms hanging loosely by his sides. His eyes stared off across the fields towards the kopje above Drew's farm. I had never seen my father looking passive; it was that, perhaps, more than anything that struck me hardest. He had always been moving, always intense. Even when he bent down close to me, to put his arms around me, I had felt the crackle of his energy. To see him so inert, swinging softly in the early morning breeze, was the strangest thing of all.

His face was grey and his eyes, normally lit with life, were faded and bulging slightly. Open wounds marked his handsome torso. His shirt had been torn off. Flies buzzed around him, reminding me of the meat hung up in the market.

My mother's hand was icy. She did not speak. Silently she gazed up at him. Around the tree women wept, ululated, cried out, but my mother did not utter a sound. When I looked up I saw that she was crying; the tears gathered in the folds of her lips. Even her weeping was silent.

'Cut him down,' she said, finally, softly. 'Cut him down and bring him home.'

I do not remember him lying on the table in our one room hut, though I know from my mother that was where they laid him. I know, also, from my mother, that I sat beneath the table the whole day long and would have lain down to sleep there that night too if she had let me.

The house was busy with neighbours and friends and family. Legs. That is what I recall, now – all the legs that passed me that day. That and the sound of women grieving. Father O'Leary came in the afternoon. He was an old man by then. He took me and stood me between his legs as he sat on one of the few chairs in our house. I remember vividly the way he looked. If I close my eyes now, I could picture him vividly. And yet my father's face is a blank. Why is that?

Father O'Leary conducted the funeral service and I stood and threw a handful of dust onto his coffin: but that was many years ago and I was a young boy and I remember nothing of it beyond that one image of him swinging from the tree.

I inherited my father's looks, but, unfortunately, not his temperament. I was a lazy child, always dreaming and Father O'Leary, although he attempted to be patient with me, and to nurture me, would often grow frustrated and chide me with comparisons with my father. I was never resentful of these reprimands; my father was a god in my eyes, a gentle spirit that hovered over me and spoke to me with my mother's voice.

Though I learned to read and write I showed no aptitude for study. I recall those days; playing football, fighting and smoking the stubs of cigarettes gathered in the streets. My mother had taken a job in the home of a white family in Bindura and I rarely saw her. Sometimes I would wake in the night to find her beside me, sitting on the edge of the bed, gazing down at me. Seeing me awake she would stroke my cheek, tears welling in her dark eyes, and though I longed for those moments with an unbearable aching of my heart, I would shrug her off and turn my back and pretend to sleep.

In those days every aspect of life was segregated. There were buses for the whites, smart affairs with seats that looked as though they must have come from some of those white people's houses. The buses for the blacks were decrepit, often without windows, billowing acrid fumes and often running out of petrol.

I recall the resentment welling on those occasional mornings when I would walk with my mother to the bus station and we would sit for some moments in the black's waiting room and watch the smart white folk, with their neat children going about their business.

'Study hard and you can change things,' my mother would tell me, when I spoke about such things, but I did not see how reading novels and Shakespeare and doing algebra would change the situation. The faces in all the books I saw were white and so were the writers and the teachers. I had no interest in it all. I finished school just as soon as I could and found work running errands for a black shopkeeper.

I was fourteen when things changed.

Working at the shop was an older youth, Joseph Charamba. Joseph was thin and lanky. He wore wire framed glasses and dressed as smartly as his poverty would allow. He was quiet and had a studious appearance and always had a book stuffed into the pocket of his jacket. For many months I ignored him, preferring the boys from my street who played football and smoked and sat at the side of the road watching girls.

When he did not arrive for work one evening, the shopkeeper cursed Joseph and told me to serve behind the counter, a long board of wood supported by sacks of rice. I was happy to take up the position, numbers were no problem for me and I could handle the change with ease. I had just got into my stride, offering an enthusiastic sales pitch to each customer that entered the dark, concrete room that served as the shop when two men struggled in carrying Joseph between them.

They laid him down on the wooden counter. His face was bloodied and his shirt ripped and covered in dirt.

'The police beat him,' one of the men panted. He

gesticulated over his shoulder, out into the bright sunlight. 'We were out in the streets… protesting… the bus strikes.' He could hardly get his words out, whether from exhaustion or fear I couldn't tell. Joseph was moaning.

'Did they hurt him bad?' the shopkeeper asked, eyeing his body nervously.

'They smacked him good with their batons.'

When the two men had gone, I helped the shopkeeper fetch a bucket of water and washed his face and checked the bruising to his sides. Joseph winced when I cleaned the blood and dirt from his skin.

'What you go doing that for, man?' I asked.

'It's important,' he said, through his teeth. 'We got to stand up to them.'

He gave me a book. New but dog-eared already, its cover almost falling from it, the spine broken from having been folded back. On the front cover it read *Kwame Nkrumah* in blue letters.

'Read this, kid,' he said, 'it's time you started learning about the world.'

I looked at it suspiciously. 'I don't know,' I said. 'I'm not so keen on books.'

'You can't read?'

'Yes, I can read,' I shot back. 'I just don't see much point in it.'

He stopped in the doorway. He had been on his way out, leaving me brushing the dust from the floor. Stepping back into the dimness of the shop, he lowered his voice.

'Listen, kid,' he said, 'there's nothing so important as books. That why they end up getting banned or burnt. Books are dangerous. You know why they're so dangerous?'

He had poked his face up close to mine. His glasses had been broken in the police charge that had knocked him senseless and he had used string to fix them back together. The glass in one of the lenses was cracked so that when you looked at his left eye it was distorted. I thought about the books I had read at the mission school and could not imagine why they would be dangerous.

'They're dangerous,' he said, prodding my chest, 'because they're full of ideas. And you know what? There's nothing more frightening for the white man than us filling our head with ideas.'

I read it that evening in the light of a small kerosene lamp, at the table in our hut, waiting for my mother to return. *Freedom is not something that one people can bestow on another as a gift*, Nkrumah wrote. *They claim it as their own and none can keep it from them.*

That book got me started. I returned it to Joseph the next day and asked him if he had anything else. He gave me Marcus Garvey. Karl Marx. In the early evenings I devoured these books as I had never any text I had read at school. I began to join Joseph and some of his friends who would meet and discuss politics, communism, revolution, black rule in Africa and for the first time in my life I drank in ideas that made sense to me, that seemed relevant to my life.

Darkness had fallen. I was sitting at the rickety table, a single candle burning, its light fluttering in the slight breeze that came from the open door. My eyes watered as I tried to read the text. I held the pages so close to the flame they almost singed. My mother had not yet returned and I was alone, restless, not tired from the day's work in the shop.

I heard their voices before the rap against the door. Closing the book, I laid it on the table and called out to them softly. Joseph's face appeared in the doorway, barely visible in the shadow cast by the curtain strung up across the room to give my mother some privacy.

'Comrade,' he said, his voice serious as it always was. 'Come with us.'

'Where are you going?'

Coming further into the room he patted the pockets of

his worn trousers. The pockets bulged, and he pulled a stone from one of them, holding it out, almost as if it was a jewel. He grinned.

'Enough of the books,' Joseph said. 'It's time for action.'

It was a dry night. The air was cool and sharp with the scent of wood smoke. The roads were quiet and we kept to the backstreets. The police station was on the edge of the town and we approached it from the back. There were six of us, young men I recognised from Joseph's meetings. Closer to the police station I noticed movements in the shadows. Warily I stepped back, but Joseph whistled short and low and a group of men paced out into the road. By the time we had skirted the low building another group had joined us and we were about twenty strong.

The police station was quiet. Electric lights glimmered dully behind the glass in the windows and, above the doorway, a bulb illuminated the dark street. A car was pulled up against the pavement. There was a sharp crack and the side window of the car shattered. For a moment I was perplexed, I had not seen the stone fly. It had come from behind me and there was a grunt of satisfaction that the first missile had hit home.

Almost immediately shadows flittered against the light inside the station. A second stone pinged off the wall, but another hit the window and that shattered too. And then we all threw our stones, fanning out across the street in a rough semi-circle and I felt a wonderful joy, a lightening of my soul, as though something heavy that had been weighing down inside me had shifted and begun to rise to the surface. I scrambled in the dust seeking more ammunition but could find only a bottle. As I threw it a head poked out from the doorway and the bottle shattered beside it so that it ducked back in again immediately.

For five minutes we pelted the police station; the men inside were trapped and had little chance to respond. Soon, though, our stones began to run out. Pockets light and empty, the young men began to scuttle around in the street for extra ammunition. The momentary lull was all the police needed. There was a sharp crack and I felt a whistle of air past my ear. For a moment I did not understand what it had been, but shortly after a second bullet ricocheted off a concrete wall, pulling away the plaster facing.

'They're firing!'

'Move it!'

A hand pushed me forward and I stumbled and fell to my knees. Around me the crowd was dispersing, feet kicking up the dirt, bodies ducking and weaving. Another shot bit into the wall behind me. I scrambled forward on all fours heading for the darkness of an alley twenty feet away. The road was suddenly, brightly illuminated so that the bricks and the broken bottles stood out in sharp relief. A car had swerved into the street and its engine gunned as it sped towards us. I felt my heart constrict with panic. Felt the adrenalin pump into my veins. I jumped up and ran. I ran faster than I had ever run, down through the alleys and the darkened back streets, tripping and falling and picking myself up and, ignorant of the cuts and the bruises. I hurdled fences, stumbled through vegetable plots until, panting, I stopped and listened to the distant sound of the sirens, the occasional crack of rifle fire and the echo of shouts in narrow streets.

It was a few nights later that I heard Mugabe. Joseph had invited me to a church where an activist was due to speak.

'It didn't put you off?' he laughed when I went to work the next day.

'Man, it was the best thing!' I whispered, so the shopkeeper would not hear. 'They were stuck, man, they couldn't move!'

'Tomorrow, come to church, there is somebody I want to hear.'

'At church?' I mocked.

'He's the leader of ZANU. He's local, a Shona, educated. A teacher.'

Mugabe was not a large man. He was quiet and reserved, standing, before the meeting started, alone at the front of the church. He was neatly dressed, very smart and there was something refined about him, something almost delicate. When he spoke his voice was considered and educated; his words, though, were coruscating, peeling away the skin of white rule. He may have looked cool and educated, but beneath he was steel.

'The whites will never accept what you are speaking of,' an elderly man objected, after he had finished speaking. 'You go too far.'

'Whether the whites accept or not is immaterial,' Mugabe responded icily. 'They will have to capitulate whether they like it or not. They will have to accept domination.'

His words thrilled me. When I listened to him I felt the anger that was squeezed deep inside me had found a voice. As I sat listening to him, I thought of my mother, of how she had whispered to me late in the night when she returned from work, stroking me gently as I pretended to sleep.

'Your father would say,' she would begin. 'Your father would say… '

Through her, then, I had learned of Nehanda. Through her I heard of Tafara and Zindonga. Of the farm that was ours before the whites came, of the herds that grazed this land, of the burial site of our elders, of the hills where the spirits of our ancestors lingered, waiting for the white man to be gone, waiting to reclaim their land. 'One day my bones will rise,' my mother cooed in the darkness. 'One day my bones will rise, and in that day the white man's bullets will turn to water and we will drive him from his land.'

Mugabe's quiet insistent voice wound itself around me. It was like flint against my soul, striking a spark. Gently he blew upon the kindling, feeding the little flame burning inside.

Later, I stood in the darkness and waited for him. He left the church alone, a book tucked beneath his arm, his head down. He stepped carefully along the path, as though attempting to keep his polished, leather shoes clean.

'Mr Mugabe, sir,' I said.

He turned sharply, and stopped.

'Yes?' he said.

I felt his eyes boring into me from behind the thick lenses of his glasses. I shifted my feet nervously, glanced down at my shoes, old, plastic sandals that slopped as I walked.

'What can I do, sir?' I whispered. 'I want to do something to help.'

He stepped closer. Examined me. I could smell his clothes, fresh, a hint of cologne. I could hear his breathing; short, shallow breaths. He raised his hand and I flinched. He hesitated a moment. I noticed a tremor run through him, like a breeze passing across the surface of water. He went to lay his hand upon my shoulder, but then seemed to change his mind and withdrew it and tapped the side of his nose thoughtfully.

'Are you afraid?' he asked.

I shook my head.

'The other night we pelted a police station,' I volunteered, glancing up at his face.

He nodded. 'You want to fight?'

'Fight?' I said.

I pictured my father swinging from the outstretched limb of the tree. Pictured the way that his eyes had stared emptily across the fields, across Drew's farm, that land that had been ours.

'Yes, sir,' I said. 'Yes, I want to fight.'

He nodded again and a faint smile flickered across his face.

'Good,' he said. 'Come and see me.'

He folded back the cover of the book and took out a small piece of paper, which he passed to me.

'You can read?'

'Yes, sir.'

He nodded again, at this, and turned and carried on walking down the path towards the main road, stepping gingerly as he went, keeping his shoes clean.

26

Roy yelled in anger. The light flashed on in the kitchen and Natalie heard him cursing. When she got there Roy was sitting on one of the stools, and blood seeped onto the floor tiles.

'Don't move!'

Natalie stopped in the doorway. The floor was covered in broken glass and on the kitchen table lay a half brick. Skirting around the table, Natalie went to the cupboard and pulled out a brush and swept up the shards and the glittering grit of glass that had scattered across the room from the broken window. A breeze blew in. Outside was the sound of movement, low mutterings, the crackle of a fire in the distance. Roy rinsed his cut heel quickly and applied some hasty bandaging.

'Bastards,' he muttered.

Leaving the light burning in the kitchen, Roy indicated for Natalie to follow him. They went out through the back of the house, down by the barn and crept past the hedges and the cottage to the fencing. Around the front of the house the light of the bonfire flickered brightly now and a large crowd of men had gathered.

'Looks like they might be getting ready for some action,' Roy said.

He glanced at his watch, it was a little after four in the morning; the sky had not begun to lighten yet, but dawn was no more than an hour away.

'My guess is that they will be ready to move in as soon as it begins to get light,' Roy said. 'Nobody likes surprises and they're going to want to see how we are going to respond. I don't think they'll move in darkness.'

They walked quietly forward across the grass to get a closer look at the crowd of men. Natalie estimated there were around thirty of them now, squatting around the fire. A few others wandered back and forth along the perimeter fence smoking. The scent of the cigarettes drifted on the light breeze.

'*Mbanje*,' Roy said. 'They're smoking marijuana.'

He signalled for Natalie to move and they doubled back around the barn to the house. In the back room, Roy stopped and gazed out of the window into the darkness.

'I don't like it,' Roy said. 'The atmosphere doesn't feel good. I don't like that they'll be high.'

He turned around and ran a hand through his grey hair.

'What are you going to do?'

Roy shook his head and sighed. He looked suddenly very weary.

'Let's wait till dawn,' he said. 'Let's see what they do. Hopefully there will be some reasoning with them.'

As he spoke the sound of voices grew louder outside. The sound of a ragged chant and the beating of drums. From the window Natalie saw lights moving around the perimeter of the fence. She felt a lurch in her chest and a sudden fear gripped her. Roy turned sharply back to the window.

'Kristine!' he shouted. 'Kristine, are you dressed?'

He moved quickly into the hall and leapt up the stairs, Natalie followed him. Roy ran down the corridor and opened the door of his bedroom. Natalie stood on the landing feeling her legs tremble. She gazed down into the stairwell where the dog stood growling softly in front of the oak doors.

A moment later Roy reappeared and behind him Kristine, dressed in jeans and a khaki shirt, her hair tied back. She must have already been dressed and ready; her jaw was set and her eyes were hard.

'Have you called the others?' she asked.

Roy shook his head. 'I'm going to phone Boyle now, see if he can get up here fast.'

The sound of chanting had grown louder and as they moved down the stairs they could hear the crunch of footsteps on the gravel path. The dog began barking, running backwards and forwards in front of the door. At the back of the hallway another door opened and the maid appeared, her face drawn with fear.

'They're coming, ma'am,' she said, turning to Kristine, her voice shaking, 'they're coming across the lawns.'

'Where are Bhekinkosi and the others?' Kristine said. Her voice was tight and controlled showing little sign of fear.

'They're out the back, ma'am. Some of them wanted to run away, they are afraid ma'am. They don't want to be beaten.'

Kristine glanced at Roy who stood in the doorway to the lounge. Roy looked back at her but seemed at a loss as to what he should suggest.

'Tell them to remain in their homes,' Kristine said, turning back to the maid. 'Tell them not to come out unless they have to. They shouldn't try to confront the men and they will be safer if they stay on the farm.'

The maid disappeared through the door into the darkness. Roy remained in the doorway.

'Do you think that is best?' he said.

'I don't know.' Kristine leaned back against the wall. 'They're probably better off running for it.'

A knock silenced them. For a moment they stood looking at the large oak door. It was not a violent banging, or even a loud knock; it was quiet, but authoritative, and in the middle of the night, above the chanting and the sound of the drums and the dog barking it seemed incongruous. Kristine's eyebrows shot up. Roy held up his hand and put a finger to his lips.

'The police?' he whispered.

He stepped over to the door and put his hand on the black, metal handle. He waited some moments, turning briefly to look at his wife. Then he opened the door.

For some moments they could see nothing. Whoever had knocked had stepped backwards into the darkness and against the glare of the light in the hallway it was not possible to see more than a couple of feet out into the garden. Roy leaned across and flicked on the outside light.

Standing alone in the sudden illumination was an elderly man, half naked, dressed on the lower half in traditional Shona costume. In his hand he held no club or primitive axe as many of the veterans did, but rather a photograph. He held it out. Natalie did not recognise him immediately, though the face and the shock of greying hair seemed familiar. Roy glanced at the photograph the old man held out.

'Moses… ' he said.

27

It was dark when we met beneath the flame tree at the top of the ridge north of Bindura. The sun had long since set. Its brief, brassy light had lit the path up over the top of the kopje as I made my way from my mother's house. As darkness descended, it began to grow cold and I shivered in my thin shirt. I glanced back only once at the flickering lights of the township and tried to make out my mother's house, a black space. My mother would not be home until much later.

For a brief moment I imagined her pushing wearily through the front door and seeing the bed empty. Pictured her face as she picked up the note I had written, scribbled rapidly on a sheet pulled from an old school exercise jotter. Steeling myself, I turned my back on her and, slouching against the wind, tramped after the shadow that was disappearing into the darkness ahead of me.

There were five other men squatting in the dust beneath the flame tree. They barely looked up as the three of us flung ourselves down on the ground beside them.

'*Kanjani*,' a stocky man in his mid-thirties said.

We nodded our heads. 'Hi.'

I glanced around timidly. I barely knew my two travelling companions. I had met them only the previous evening in a house on the edge of Bindura. Mugabe had been there, sat primly on a wooden chair by the table, a book under the palm of his hand, that serious look on his face. He had introduced us, had given us instructions on where to meet. We used code names: Lion, Desert Dog and Gazelle. I was Gazelle, 'Swift and young,' Mugabe said looking at me with his intense eyes.

For an hour we sat there, shivering, barely saying a word. At one point one of the young men took out the butt of a cigarette and lit it.

'Put it out,' the stocky man hissed.

The youth looked up and for a moment I noted the defiant crease of his brow as though he was about to argue, but then he thought better of it and stubbed it out carefully in the dust and put it back into the pocket of his shirt. It was after midnight when the sound of a low whistle broke the silence and the stocky man pricked up his ears and motioned to us.

We moved out quickly, sliding over the edge of the ridge, keeping low, so that our silhouettes would not be noticed against the clear, star-studded night sky. For some miles we followed a ravine that ran down the side of the hill and then, fording it, the water rushing around our knees, we cut north and headed off across the grassland keeping in single-file, not saying a word.

The young smoker was ahead of me, and I noticed how often his hand would fly up to his pocket to extract the cigarette. He would bring it up to his nose and inhale the stale scent of it deeply. Then carefully poke it back into his shirt.

It was almost dawn when we crept up the side of a rocky escarpment and crawled into a narrow fissure in the rock, barely wider than our thin bodies, and crouched down. The sky lightened rapidly, and before long it was day. The heat rose with the sun and the cool moisture of the night quickly evaporated. My stomach ached with hunger and my legs were worn sore. Resting my head against the rock behind me, I fell into a dazed slumber, waking occasionally, my neck aching and my bones crying out to lay flat against the earth, but there was not space.

Sometime later a bottle of water was passed along the line and we all drank from it thirstily. There was bread too, a crust that you could only nibble at, it was so dry; but it kept the worst of the hunger at bay.

When it grew dark, we moved on again, and the second night was harder than the first. The young man dropped behind me, and I heard the scratch of a match and a moment later the scent of his cigarette. Turning I could see little, he had it cupped tight within his hands, so tight it must have been burning them.

'Hey,' I said, dropping behind.

'What?' he shot back, his voice sullen and tight with aggression.

'Give me a drag, or I'll shout up front.'

'You shout and I'll knock every tooth out of your mouth,' he said, but he quickly handed me the stub and I inhaled the hot smoke greedily.

It was on the third morning that we crossed the border. A small village clung to the side of a hill and as the sun rose we staggered up the low incline and collapsed among the ragged huts.

A few days later a truck picked us up and we drove to a camp deep in the bush. There were about fifty men at the camp, some of them little older than me, grizzled men in their thirties, dressed in rags, thin and with eyes haunted by hunger, and one who was younger, a boy of no more than fourteen.

The food we got in the camp was basic, but it was probably better than what most of us were used to. We were given a uniform too, khaki clothes that didn't fit. We trained hard and in the evenings, exhausted, we gathered in the huts to listen to political instruction; Marxism, visions of an Africa liberated from imperial white control, united, free. The English gone. Once Mugabe came to a meeting. He watched us as we paraded in the dust, stood bolt upright, shaded by an umbrella he held delicately in his soft scholar's hands.

It's hard to explain how much we idolised Mugabe – he was something we had not seen before, an educated African, smart, knowledgeable, cultured and with a deep, bitter, visceral hatred of the colonial powers. He had no fear of the white man, he taught us to spit in their faces.

Most of the lectures in the evenings were dry and pedantic and often I would fall to sleep, buried away in the corner, but when Mugabe came, my eyes were wide. He could have spoken all night and I would not have slept. If I had felt my eyelids closing, I would have ripped them off, but they never closed. He filled the air with an electric current. I was ready to die for him.

I grew up there, on that camp. Physically I grew stronger, but it wasn't just that, nor the passing of the months, the year, the slow turn from the blistering, dry weather in August when we set out from Bindura, through the rains, the hot sultry days with their sudden downpours, when we would emerge from treks through the bush soaked through to the skin, and then the cool weather, dry and temperate. I learned to carry a gun, to fire it. And I learned there, in that dusty camp, to focus the burning inarticulate rage I had felt ever since I could remember, ever since I had seen my father hanging from a tree. I learned to hate. To hate enough to kill.

It was the day after we heard that Mugabe had been arrested that we finally moved out of the camp, in small groups, and began our journey back to the border. The evening the news arrived I walked up out of the camp, and climbed to the top of a low hill. The ground was rocky and bare and there was a good view over the surrounding countryside. It reminded me of the kopje behind our old farm, where my mother had taken me to see the grave of my great-grandfather Chimukoko. We had stood in the cool silence of the grave and my mother had poured out a jug of beer on the hard-packed earth floor.

'*Mudzimu*,' she breathed, 'spirits hear!'

I stood by her side trembling in the still darkness.

'Guide your son,' she whispered, rocking backwards and forwards, 'have mercy upon him.'

A low ululation broke from her lips, a haunting, grieving sound that rose and rose and sent a chill down my spine as it echoed around the walls of the cave. I looked up and saw her staring eyes roll back. She faced the ceiling, the veins stood out on her throat and the noise rose.

'*Amai*!' I called, gripping her arm.

At that moment a shadow darkened the entrance of the cave and I cried out and fell to the ground.

'What the hell are you doing here?' the red haired apparition bellowed, his voice drowning out that of my mother's.

Amai stopped and turned and I saw a sudden look of fear and something else flash across her face. Reginald Drew lifted his arm and it was only then that I saw that he was carrying a rod, a thick stick he had been using to walk with. He swung it hard and it hit my mother across her side. She cried out and fell to the earth. He lifted it again and I screamed as it fell, unable to move, unable to save my mother from its blow.

'Get out, get off my land,' the white man screamed, thrashing at my mother with his stick.

Crawling and grunting, arm raised above her head to ward off the blows, she grabbed my hand and we scrambled through the beery dirt, out of the cave. Sobbing and howling we staggered down the hillside. Snot bubbled from my nose. Only at the bottom of the path did we pause and look back up to see Drew standing there in the entrance to the cave, a tall, wiry man, his white skin almost as red as his short cropped hair, still brandishing his stick.

Kare kare. That was how she always started. Long, long ago. Late into the night, when she came home and sat on the bed beside me she told me the stories of my father, of Tafara, my grandfather, and of his father before him, the unbroken line of men who had farmed the land beneath the kopje and hunted in the woods that surrounded it, who had raised cattle there, had married and borne sons.

Kare kare. Long ago now. They seemed little more than fairy tales.

As I lay on the rocks staring up into the star-studded night I longed for her tales, for her stories of the land that had existed before the white man came.

We left the camp in small groups, each with a commander, an older soldier who had already been involved in guerrilla activities. Trekking south we reached the shores of the Zambezi at the end of the second day and when darkness fell we took a small wooden boat, which we paddled as silently as we were able across the waters.

Working south, following a narrow, winding river, we joined up with a small detachment in a village north of Chinhoyi. From there we travelled west, moving only at night through the fertile farm land. Dogs barked, and occasionally a white farmer ventured out, rifle cocked and let off a few shots into the darkness, and I would feel my heart thump as we waded along the bed of the shallow stream, our heads low.

Late one evening we entered a village in the Dande region. Smoke hung low over the village and from several huts could be seen the faint flickering of firelight. We spread out between the huts and shouted out, slapping our hands against the crumbling mud walls.

'Out, out.'

The villagers crept out of the buildings, faces tight with fear. We collected them together in the centre of the huts and built up a fire. The chief of the village was an old man. His bald head reflected the light of the fire as if it has been polished. The younger children huddled close to the legs of their mothers. As I stood there, with the old rifle flung across my shoulder, I felt a power I had never felt before. And a pride too.

The commander of our group stepped forward.

'Forward with ZANU!' he shouted.

The villagers gawped at him silently.

'You must answer, "forward!" the commander told them. He tried it again, calling out loudly.

'Forward!' the villagers replied obediently.

Behind the legs of the women some of the children grinned at the sudden chanting.

'Do you know who we are?' the commander asked. 'We are the spirits of Zimbabwe. For many years the white people have taken our land. They have forced us from our farms and away from the lands of our ancestors. They drove us onto barren reserves, while they themselves took the best of what was left. They beat us and imprison us.

'Well, no longer. The spirit of Nehanda has returned. 'My bones will rise again,' she said. We are the bones of Nehanda risen from the soil of our land, come to reclaim it.'

Later we taught them songs we had learned in the training camps. *'We come to free Zimbabwe, grandmother Nehanda, ancestral, spirits of war.'*

For some months we stayed in those villages in the north of the country, living first in one village, teaching the young people, recruiting new fighters who were sent across the border for training, then moving to neighbouring areas. But as I lay down each night, I longed to move south, to go back to the valleys around Bindura, back to where my ancestors land had been. In truth, when the time came to move from recruitment to fighting, I knew which white face I wanted to seek out. I knew in whose body my first bullet would lodge.

One morning, Hopeful called us together. Hopeful was the commander of our small group. He was a thin man with an odd shaped face and beneath his pinched, small forehead, a large nose bulged out. We squatted around him and watched as he took a stick and drew out a crude map of the area in the dirt. When he had finished he pointed to a cross he had drawn.

'After the disaster at Sinoia,' he said, 'when seven of our fighters were killed, a spirit of dismay fell upon us. We threw ourselves forward and such was our enthusiasm that we imagined that nothing could hold us back.'

I nodded eagerly. I felt that Hopeful did not like me. He was slightly shorter than I was, and often he would throw off a snide remark about my looks.

'But like our fathers and our grandfathers,' he continued, 'we must learn not to take literally *Mabuya* Nehanda's words. The bullets will not turn to water. They will not dissolve in the air. She was speaking in metaphors. But now, after two years, we move.'

We left the village early the next morning and for three days were journeyed south. We kept to the thick bush, well away from the farms and the roads. Occasionally light planes or helicopters soared over and we crouched in the dirt, like animals, and waited and watched in silence until they had gone. At night we built small fires to keep the wild animals at bay. Each day the country around us grew more familiar, more like home.

As we moved into the Bindura valley, I pushed ahead, I knew the pathways and the caves where we could hide and took pleasure in leading the small group. Hopeful lagged behind. He looked reticent and wary. Our orders had come through and we were to dynamite a railway line and attack a military station. Our job was to cause as much mayhem as we could and then withdraw quickly back towards the border with Mozambique.

Ours was one of a number of attacks that had been coordinated by the ZANLA leadership, most of whom were in prison. The attacks were to be as close to the capital, Salisbury, as possible, as symbolic gestures intended to strike fear into the heart of Ian Smith's government.

Hopeful, I knew, thought the idea reckless. He thought that it would be another Sinoia. We had argued about it long into the night. I cared little about the reasons, or the military campaign that Chitepo, Mugabe and the others were waging. I had my own personal battle to fight.

It was as we worked down the valley, moving slowly and only after dark that the incident happened.

The sun had not yet risen, but the air glowed with its approach. The bush was shrouded with a pale blue haze. We had been walking through the night and were tired. Stepping out into a small clearing we stumbled suddenly upon a girl collecting water from a stream.

The girl was young, no more than thirteen. She had a thin, athletic frame and a pretty face. Her dress was old and frayed and slipped from her shoulder. She cried out, alarmed, as we stepped out of the brush. The bucket at her feet toppled over and the water spilled out across the sandy earth, darkening it. We stopped dead in our tracks and for a moment we were all silent.

'What's your name, sister?' Hopeful said.

He walked across to her, his gun swinging by his side. The girl's eyes widened with fear. It was possible to see her lips tremble. She bent forward on her knees into a position of supplication. Hopeful stopped in front of her and stood for a moment in silence looking down at the girl. He lifted his boot and put it beneath the girl's chin, tilting her face up.

'What's your name, sister?'

The girl breathed so hard that her thin chest rose and fell like that of a wounded deer. I felt my heart contract. It was impossible not to feel her fear. I glanced around at the men, they were laughing. But I saw something else too; something in their eyes. The way that their tongues ran over their lips.

Hopeful raised his foot forcing the girl's face up and then he kicked her and she sprawled backwards against the wet earth, her body twisting away from Hopeful, her torn dress riding up her leg revealing the bottom of her small buttocks. She made no sound.

'Hopeful!'

I stepped forward. I had intended to speak with a loud and commanding voice, but when I heard it, it sounded weak and trembling. He turned, a grin on his face.

'Comrade,' he said. 'Brother, you want to be first?'

His hand swooped in an elegant flourish, indicating the prone girl. I glanced down at her. Her face was buried in the sand, her fists clamped. Behind me the men were laughing. Hopeful reached out with the barrel of his rifle and pushed the girl's dress higher. He did not look down at the child, his eyes bored into me.

'Leave her,' I said. 'Let her be, she's just a child.'

'Are you going to stop me?'

I stiffened. Behind me the men had stopped laughing. I felt their eyes on my back. Hopeful raised the rifle, his finger sliding across the smooth, worn wood of the stock towards the trigger. I tried to laugh, but the sound that came out was sickly.

'Come on,' I said. 'She's too young. Leave her be. That's not what we came here for.'

Hopeful stepped towards me. His face creased with annoyance. He was sweating and he stank of the marijuana we had been smoking as we marched. He pushed the rifle barrel up into my face; the metal dug into my skin and cracked against my teeth. I stepped back and pushed it away with my hand. Hopeful laughed. He threw the gun to one of the men behind me and then carefully and deliberately he took hold of the buckle of his belt and began to undo it.

I moved past him and stood beside the girl. She cowered away from me. Taking the rifle from my shoulder I held it ready at my side.

'Enough,' I said.

Hopeful's trousers fell to the floor. I looked to the others behind him. Their faces seemed suddenly alien and twisted. Brutal. They moved forward, a hand reaching out and pushing me in the chest, forming a semi-circle around the girl. For a moment I struggled, tussling with the men, then I stepped back.

Hopeful was trying to take hold of the girl, but she began to resist, her body writhing and her legs kicking. He slapped her hard which momentarily stunned her, but as he tried to mount her again, she screamed and bit him and scratched at his face with her nails.

Again I jumped forward to pull him off her, but the men formed a circle, pushing me out. A foot shot out and kicked the girl in the head. She moaned and lay still. I took the rifle and shot a single round over the heads of the men.

The noise of the gunshot reverberated from the granite face of the valley wall. From the trees the birds rose in screaming clouds. The air was a sudden cacophony of sound contrasting with the abrupt silence of the men. Hopeful stood, slowly, pulling his trousers up, and fastening his belt. He held out his hand to one of the men for his gun, but I shook my head.

'No!'

I pointed the rifle at the men. Hopeful's hand fell back down by his side and the men shuffled back. I knelt down by the side of the girl and eased her head up on to my lap. A thin trickle of blood slipped down her cheek from a cut beneath her eye, but she was conscious. Her mouth was bloody too.

Before I could speak we all heard the noise of the engine gunning, coming close. Startled, the men fled, crashing through the bushes and dense undergrowth. The vehicle stopped and doors slammed. A few moments later a white man burst into the small clearing, behind him two farm hands. I recognised him at once. His flaming red hair.

Seeing me and the girl on my lap, the men stopped. For a moment the rifle in my hand remained pointed into the air, but then I dropped it and held up my hands. The girl moaned and clung to me.

'I know you,' Reginald Drew said.

His angry red face poked forward and he examined me. He seemed to be searching around in his brain and then he tapped his forehead.

'You're the son of Zindonga. Moses,' he said triumphantly.

'That's it – Moses.'

I gazed at him astonished.

28

Seeing Moses, something in Natalie's chest lifted and she noticed that this was the same in Roy and in Kristine. Kristine smiled and looked so relieved Natalie thought she would cry.

Moses did not move beyond the doorstep. He pointed at the photograph held out in his hand. 'Look at it,' he said. His voice was neither aggressive nor friendly. He spoke loudly and clearly, as if he was determined to make a point.

Roy glanced down at the photograph and then back up at Moses and beyond into the darkness.

'Do you want to come in?' he said.

Moses glanced at the open doorway, at the lit hallway and Kristine and Natalie. A strange look passed across his face and he shook his head.

'Look at the photograph,' he repeated.

Behind him torches moved across the lawn and the sound of singing filled the late night air. There was no sign of dawn. The sky was ponderously dark. The scent of smoke was heavy in the air. At Roy's feet the dog stood snarling, its hackles raised. Distracted, Roy stepped forward out onto the gravel.

'What are they doing?' he asked. 'Why have they got the torches?'

A frown creased Moses' large forehead and his lips twisted

slightly. He pushed Roy as he stepped back, surprised. He held his hands up as if in a gesture of surrender. Other faces appeared, swimming up out of the darkness; dull faces, men whose opened shirts displayed scarred, sweat-glistening bodies. The scent of marijuana clung to them. Their eyes were wild. They gathered around the back of Moses, glaring into the neat farmhouse, machetes and home-made axes hanging loosely from hands.

'Look at the photograph,' Moses said, enunciating each word carefully, slowly, his voice hard and determined.

Roy glanced down at the photograph again, but his eyes would not hold it, they glanced back up at the men that were closing in around the entry to the house. Kristine stepped forward and stood beside him. She took the photograph from Moses and looked at it.

'What is it Moses?' she asked.

Moses breathed heavily, nodding as if it justified something, as though by looking at it they would understand. He said nothing. Kristine glanced up at him and then back down at the old brown piece of card that she held.

'It's awfully old,' she said.

Roy bent his head to look over her shoulder and then he took the photograph and studied it himself. His finger traced the figures on the image. He glanced up again at Moses and Natalie could see that he did not understand what Moses wanted from him.

'Who is it of?' he asked.

'Ahh,' said Moses, as if suddenly they were getting somewhere. 'Who are they? Who are they?' He nodded and smiled coldly. 'Indeed, that is the question, is it not? That's what needs to be asked.' He looked at the men who drifted around him, as if they too were a part of this bizarre conversation but they milled sullenly, and seemed uninterested.

A man carried a torch, a crude stick tied with a rag soaked in oil, the flames dancing from it. He walked over to the house, a thick acrid smoke trailing behind him. He looked stoned. Peering at Roy and Kristine he laughed. He held up the torch and thrust it quickly beneath the thatch of the porch. Kristine let out a short, sharp cry and Roy jumped forward, the photograph fluttering out of his hands and landing on the gravel as he lunged for the torch, grabbing the man's arm and pushing him away.

'Are you mad?' he screamed at the man.

A group of them closed in around him. Their faces leapt in the light of the flames, so that noses and eyes seemed to swim loosely back and forth across their faces. The torch swooped around and was pushed close to Roy's angry, frustrated face.

'Roy!' Kristine screamed.

Moses bent down and picked up the photograph and thrust it back at Roy. He pushed the others away, shooing them off.

'Look,' he said.

'What is it Moses?' Roy said impatiently.

Roy turned around to face Moses who was smaller than he was and looked down at him, taking in the wild grey hair, the bare old chest, sunken with age, the tribal costume. He smiled, perhaps seeing the slightly ridiculous nature of the situation. Moses stepped back and spat at him – a thick goblet that landed on Roy's shoes.

Roy was startled. He looked down at his shoe and then at Moses.

'Moses!' Kristine exclaimed.

'Here,' Moses thrust the photograph up close to Roy's face. 'Here in this picture you should see, you should understand,' he said. 'These people, do you know who they are? They are my ancestors. This here, my grandfather… ' His finger pointed at the face. 'Tafara.' He held up the photo again so that Roy could identify the man. 'This here was his wife. And where are they? They are standing right here,' he pointed at his feet, at the gravel path, and then he waved his hand taking in the land around them. 'Here!'

At that moment the first streaks of light began to temper

the darkness of the night. A ghostly hue hung over the dimly perceivable ridge behind the farm, as though by the stretch of his arm Moses had begun to reveal the land to them. And that was how his face looked: triumphant.

'This was their land,' he said, 'Tafara's land, and before him his father's and before his father... ' he paused, and threw out his arm again to indicate the passage back through time, 'his father. Our fathers lived here, farmed here. It was our land.'

He grabbed hold of Roy's arm and yanked him forward out of the porch and its light. Kristine yelped with fright. The light was coming on fast now, so that the ridge and Drew's Kopje stood out suddenly stark against the growing day. Moses pointed up to it. The brush around it glowed with a strange energy and then, a moment later, the top boulder flared, lighting up like a beacon against the dark canvas of the fading night.

'There,' he said, 'you see that?'

Roy nodded.

'You know what is up there?'

'It's Drew's Kopje,' Roy said faintly, the words dying away as he said them, as his uncle's name, the family name, imprinted upon this landscape sounded suddenly strangely discordant in the blossoming light.

'Drew's Kopje!' Moses spat, ironically. 'There, up on that ridge, my grandfather is buried. And his father too. That is the home of our ancestral spirits. This is our land, our home.' He spun round, his face close up against Roy's. 'And you know why my father is not buried there?'

'Your father?' Roy echoed weakly.

'My father,' Moses nodded. 'Zindonga.'

He stepped back from Roy and a sudden wash of sadness changed the features of his face. For some moments he stood there gazing up at the ridge, at the sudden, vivid brilliance of dawn, as though seeing something else. When he turned back to Roy the light seemed to have left his eyes and he seemed suddenly tired and older.

'They took him. Drew took him and hanged him.' He waved his arm down across the valley. 'On a tree down there, when I was a little boy.' He gazed into Roy's face, seeing there, perhaps, the faint shadow of Reginald Drew's features. 'Drew wouldn't allow my father to be buried with his father in the sacred place.'

From the shadows of the lawn another man approached; a tall, thin man, his shirt loose, his trousers ragged around his bare feet. He stopped beside Moses and placed a hand upon his shoulder. Roy recognised him, as did Natalie.

'Your papers have been served, Drew,' the man said. 'We are taking the farm.'

'You can't,' Roy said weakly, 'you can't do that.'

The man laughed. Most of the teeth in his mouth were missing and when he laughed his gums looked black and swollen.

'On Monday I will be contacting my lawyer,' Roy said.

'On Monday you can do as you wish. You have five hours to leave the farm. If you don't go,' he let the threat hang in the air and then he nodded towards Kristine, or perhaps it had just been towards the house. 'I can't guarantee your safety after that.'

29

So how does this story end, after so many years? Even my own youth seems like an ancient tale these days.

Kare kare.

There was a look in Drew's eyes as he stared down at me, the girl's bloody head on my lap. Maybe I imagined it. Maybe I imagine it now, but as he looked at me I could see the image of my father swaying from the tree and I knew – knew without a shadow of a doubt – that it had been he who was responsible for Zindonga's death.

His face paled, as though he saw that I knew. It was the only time I had ever seen the man lost. His decisiveness seemed to leave him for a second.

'Shall we take him, *bhasa*?'

Drew glanced around at the two men by his side as if he had forgotten they were there. He held up his hand. Wait. And in that pause I took my opportunity. The gun still lay by my side and I raised it and fired.

The recoiling gun hit the girl in my lap and she jumped and screamed, knocking me off balance, and a moment later they were on me, the two men, wrestling me while I kicked and screamed like an evil spirit.

But in that moment I recalled Tafara; how he brought the rock down heavily on the head of the white soldier, right at the beginning of my story, killing him, and a wave of joy washed over me – righteous, holy joy. That was how this story should end. I, Moses, the good-for-nothing son of Zindonga had killed Drew. My only regret in that moment was that I was so young, that I had no son of my own, nobody who would take possession of this land once again.

As I turned my head to look in triumph at Drew's body, I felt a sharp, hard blow to my head and the light dimmed and slowly, slowly the sounds of the world, the girl crying, the men drifted away into the distance and I embraced the darkness.

When I came to, I was lying on the floor of a truck which lurched and jolted along the uneven dirt road. My head – my whole body – throbbed. Each movement of the truck caused a spasm of excruciating pain to shoot down my spine. I was thrown that night into a dark, crowded cell.

I was sentenced to ten years. At first I was in Salisbury prison, but then later I was moved out to Gonakudzingwa, the arid plain, a parched and desolate place. They knew that if you tried to run from there you wouldn't last the night.

When I was released I went home to live with my mother and worked at odd jobs. My mother was getting old and often she lay in her bed, too sick to move. The pittance I brought in did little to pay for food, never mind any care for her. One night she called me to sit by her.

She pressed a photograph into my hands. It was black and white, very old. In front of some mud huts a whole line of people stared into the camera, children blurred among their feet. My mother eased herself up on the bed and pointed to the figure standing in the middle of the group, a tall, thin young man, good-looking and confident, a smile playing at the edges of his lips.

'That is your grandfather,' she said, 'Tafara.'

She fell back against the thin sheet, exhausted from the

exertion of sitting up. I gazed at the figure in the photograph, traced my finger around the contours of him.

'The photograph was taken on the farm, before the white men took it,' my mother said.

'One day we will get the farm back,' I promised her.

She laughed. Her laugh was hollow and sad and I could see that she did not believe it. Did not believe things would ever change. She closed her eyes and breathed out a long sigh as if she was letting go of things, and then she was still. I shook her arm and she opened her eyes.

'Go to school, child,' she whispered.

For a moment I thought she was confused; that the years had slipped away for her and I was young again. But she fixed me with her eyes and they were clear and bright and sharp.

'It's only by being educated that we will beat them. We have to be better than them. Your father knew that.'

Two days later she asked for the priest and I fetched him. He was a small man who walked with a limp. I had never liked him. His obsequious manner and 'refined' etiquette, like he was trying to be a white man. As he knelt down on the dirt floor of our home beside my mother's bed, I stood in the corner and watched. Her mumbled confession was too quiet for me to hear and I could not think of what she would have to confess, this woman who had done nothing in her life but worked.

'This is the Lamb of God who takes away the sins of the world,' the priest muttered as he presented her with a fragment of the host.

'Lord I am not worthy to receive you,' my mother said.

When the priest stood up I was crying. He put his hand on my shoulder as he left and that made me angry, because he thought it was his superstitions that had moved me. My mother died in the early hours of the morning. I was sleeping on the floor by her bed.

After her burial I tried to do as she had asked. I went as far as enrolling on a course at the university but on the day that I was supposed to start I went to a bar and got drunk.

The bar was dirty. A couple of old men sat slumped in one of the corners in semi-darkness. The floor was earth and the bar little more than a piece of wood stood on sacks and a beer keg. As I sat there, the beer in my hands, I felt the anger rising within me.

What had Mugabe done? What had any of them done, with their English degrees and their smart suits? Yes, we had a black president now, black politicians, but what else had changed? Nothing. The whites still had the best jobs, they owned the industry. They still had all the best land, nothing had been done about that. While black farmers scratched a living on the barren reserves they had been pushed onto, the whites exploited the beautiful arable land.

'Give me another,' I said to the boy behind the bar.

I fished in my pocket for the last money I had. Pulling it out, I glanced at it and laughed. Mugabe's face stared out at me stonily.

'Here boy,' I said, wafting the crumpled note in front of his nose. 'This is what we fought for. This was what it was all about, those years of struggle, prison; so that we could have a black face on our bank notes.'

The boy took the note from me cautiously.

When I staggered down to the ZANU PF offices they were locked. I banged on the large wooden doors.

'When are you going to do something?' I bellowed. 'When are you going to give me my land back?'

At the edge of town I thumbed a lift from a truck and travelled up the valley towards the farm. The day was hot and there was no shade from the sun on the back of the truck. I had eaten little and was drunk still from the beer and when the driver dropped me off near Drew's farm I was weak and exhausted. I collapsed at the side of the road.

For some time I was out cold, sprawled in the dust. I woke to the sound of an engine. A Land Rover pulled up beside me and I heard the sound of voices. White voices. My head pounded and when I tried to open my eyes they were bleary and I could see little.

'Is he alive?'

'Stay in the car, Kristine.'

I felt something prodding me. I moaned and rolled away.

'Get some water,' the man called.

'Where from?'

'There's some in the back for the dog.'

The woman was young, no more than twenty-five. She was attractive, with shoulder length blonde hair and blue eyes. She carried a baby in her arms. Opening up the back of the Land Rover, she took out a bottle and passed it to her husband who was crouched over me.

'Drink some of this,' the man said.

I drank thirstily, the water spilling out over my lips and chin, only half of it going down my throat and that then choked me, so that I was coughing and spluttering. The man laughed.

'You'll live,' he said. 'He's just drunk,' he said to the woman, screwing the top onto the bottle and handing it back to her. 'I'll send the boy down to get him and take him up to Pasi. Somebody there'll look after him until he sobers up.'

The 'boy' was in his eighties. He walked slowly and spoke to me kindly. Thin blue films obscured his eyes.

'Cataracts,' he explained. 'I haven't been able to see for years.'

'Who was the white man?' I asked.

'The white man?' The old man chuckled. 'That would be Roy Drew, the owner of the farm.'

'Is that old man Drew's son?'

'No, his nephew. Old Drew didn't have any children as far as I know. That was before my time, I'm not from around here. Ten years or more ago Drew died, back in the seventies. Roy came over from England.'

Pasi was a small village just over the ridge, no more than five huts, the roof of one had half collapsed. A couple of families lived there, scraping a living from some rough land at the back of the village.

'You sober up, you could ask if there is work up at the farm,' the old man said thoughtfully when he left me there. 'Drew's a good farmer, he always needs more hands. He isn't bad.'

I shook my head. 'I don't think so.'

'As you like,' said the old man.

After a while he left me and I lay back on the straw bed of the one of the huts. My head throbbed and I felt nauseous. Laying there I recalled the years in prison; the chains constantly rubbing and chaffing the wrists and ankles until large calluses developed. The frustration and fear and the beatings. I looked into my heart and all I could find was darkness and anger, and that made me hate them more, that I had been reduced to this, that my life was defined by anger and hatred. Solely that; there was no other meaning.

The next morning a young woman woke me. She was a plump girl, little more than sixteen or seventeen with bright, playful eyes. She brought me water in a can and *sadza*. She sat by me, close to my feet, as I ate.

The *sadza* was good and gave me strength and I recovered quickly. The girl's father was going out into the field and I went with him and helped him to thank him for having given me shelter. There was a view from the fields, down over the valley. Lower down the slope there were some buildings and beyond that the river. Though the land was poor and it was hard to scratch something from it, I felt a sense of peace in the village and that night I slept there again.

When I awoke in the morning the girl was there once more with my water and *sadza*.

Roy came to the village the next day to see how I was. I had just sat down on a bench outside one of the huts when he drew up in the Land Rover. He was a young man, fit and lean, but fair haired and nothing like his uncle.

'How you doing today?' he asked, his accent odd; English with only the hint of the inflections of the local accent he had picked up over the ten years in the country.

I nodded. 'I'm fine.'

He stood in front of me for a while and I think he thought I might thank him, and when I didn't, he didn't seem to know what to say.

'I thought you were dead at first,' he said.

I nodded slowly.

'What's your name?' he asked.

And I saw no reason to lie to him. 'Moses,' I said.

'Well, Moses,' he said, 'if you ever need a job, I'm always looking for extra hands.'

I said nothing. He turned away then, just as the girl was coming out of one of the huts. The sun fell on her shoulder and her skin gleamed golden. Roy glanced over her and the look in his eye, proprietorial, caused a spasm of fury to rise in me. I half rose, but he had turned away already and was on his way over to his car.

The girl's name was Miriam and we were married after the rains. The next year she gave birth to the first of our daughters and then ten years later to our second. I had no sons.

Over the years, Roy would drop in at the village from time-to-time. Often it would be as he was on his way down to the school at the bottom of the valley where the teacher was politically active, a member of the MDC. Roy knew the weather was changing; that Mugabe, now that he had consolidated power for himself, was becoming less cautious. The economy was difficult. Things were getting tougher for everybody, but the whites weren't stupid. They were putting their money on Tsvangirai and the MDC. Get them in power, they thought, and their position was safe. I made sure that the local ZANU PF office knew all about the teacher and in one of the raids they took him.

As the years passed the only thing that sustained me was the photograph of Tafara and the stories I had heard from my mother. I believed those stories. I believed that Nehanda's bones would rise, that finally the white man would be driven from the land and it would be ours again.

In many ways my granddaughter, Memories, became to me the son that I did not have. I would take her up to the ridge and tell her the stories my mother had told me. Tell her about Chimukoko and Tafara, and Zindonga and the land that had been ours. She was upset, of course, when the school closed down, but I gave her other dreams.

'The time is coming,' I told her. 'I can feel it, it is coming close now. The land will be ours again and our ancestral spirits will return to their own land.'

Memories looked at me silently, those large eyes of hers boring into my soul.

'Just you see,' I whispered. 'Just you see.'

30

It was at that moment that a trail of cars sped up the road, headlights blazing and pulled up at the gates of the farm. Boyle jumped down from the front vehicle, a green Land Rover Defender. There were four more jeeps pulled up behind and moments later these, too, had disgorged their passengers. Dogs ran loose, barking and snarling viciously. Boyle carried a gun. He held it at waist height with both hands. His face was dark with anger.

Boyle let out a loud bellow. His face was red and contorted as he marched through the farm gates. The men followed after him; each carried a gun and the dogs ran around their heels growling and barking. The veterans shrank back from Boyle and his men as they approached the house.

Roy stepped forward to greet Boyle, Kristine followed behind. As he moved past Moses, Roy's shoulder caught the old man's, knocking him off balance. Moses fell to the floor, the photograph crumpling in his hand.

'Roy,' Natalie called.

One of the veterans shouted out angrily. Someone waved a machete and another veteran ran up from the fire brandishing a flaming torch. Lights danced across the front of the farm. The first rays of sun lanced across the landscape, the headlights shone through the gates, the firelight flickered.

Moses looked down at the photograph in his hands. Natalie stepped forward and bent down beside him.

'Are you hurt?' she asked.

Moses did not reply.

A gunshot startled Natalie. Her head shot up and she quickly scanned the scene. Boyle continued up the drive, the men and dogs behind him, his rifle pointed up in the air and it was clear that it was he that had fired.

The veterans began to shout. Running with the torch towards the cottage the man tossed it, flaming, onto the thatched roof. Natalie screamed. Roy and Kristine spun around and saw her on the floor beside Moses. Kristine turned back, but Natalie pointed towards the roof of the house. As Kristine glanced up towards the roof, one of the veterans ran forward, his machete glinting in the light and Kristine, seeing him coming for her, dropped to her knees on the gravel drive.

Natalie watched as if in slow motion. She was aware of the thudding of her heart and the sound of the shouting, though this seemed suddenly distant. The machete rose high above the head of the veteran, catching as it did so a ray of early morning sunlight so that it seemed to flame in his hand. Kristine's arms rose above her head. A scream formed on Natalie's lips, but she was a silent witness.

Boyle leapt forward, barreling into the man.

Natalie exhaled sharply as the two men fell to the ground. Beside her Moses was groaning in the dirt. Natalie reached out and looped her arm under his, pulling him to his feet. Moses clung onto the photograph, bent and torn in his hands. He seemed dazed.

Boyle pinned the veteran to the floor as Roy dashed over and picked up his wife from the gravel, worry etched across his face. As he straightened, he glanced up and noticed the thin column of smoke that rose in the still air from the thatch roof of the farm.

'Fire!'

Moses looked around. The sun had risen and the farm was

bathed in the warm light of dawn. The place was in chaos, with men tousling and shouting on all sides and dogs barking. On the gravel Christopher Moyo, the chairman of the local branch of the War Veterans, lay flat with a large, red-haired man straddling his chest. Moyo was shouting incoherently, waving his arms. Natalie stood at his side talking to him, but the words did not register.

'Fire!' Roy was shouting.

Moses looked up. The pillar of smoke that rose from the roof of the farmhouse was thick and acrid. A thin smile spread across his face.

A couple of the white men had dashed around the side of the house and a few moments later they hurried back, rolling out a thick hose that squirmed over the lawn. The thatch crackled loudly. Yellow flames jumped into the clear sky. All eyes had turned to the farmhouse. Boyle climbed off Christopher Moyo while Roy stood like a statue, his hands on his head, mouth open. Beside him Kristine's face was covered with her hands. Moses thought that perhaps she was screaming. Somebody was screaming.

The jet of water arced into the air and fell down upon the thatch. The smoke billowed more thickly, the column broken, spreading across the lawn in front of the house so that soon they were coughing and choking.

Kristine ran for the front door of the house, but Roy chased after, pulling her away.

'The dog,' she was shouting. 'The dog is still in the house.'

Moses bent down. At his feet was a small rock. Somebody must have thrown it, as it lay incongruously on the neatly clipped green grass. He straightened, cradling the rock in his hand. Roy was stood beside him shouting to the two men with the hose, directing them. Moses looked at him. There was no hint of red in Roy's hair, in fact there was very little resemblance in the man to Old Drew at all and yet this was his nephew, this tall, thin man that stood beside him. The stone was the size of the palm of his hand. It was smooth and heavy. He found himself weighing it, considering. His hand rose, the fingers clenching the stone. Roy turned to him and for a moment they looked into each other's eyes.

'*Sekuru*!'

The voice reached him as if from a very great distance.

'*Sekuru*!'

A figure was running across the lawn towards him. Moses lowered his hand and turned. Natalie was beside him, squeezing between him and Roy, her hands reaching out.

'Memories!' she shouted.

And suddenly the spell was broken. Moses shook his head. The sound came flooding in; the sound of the shouting, the crackle of the flames, the hiss of the water on the burning roof. Memories was charging at him. Slowly, he opened his fingers and the stone dropped from his grasp onto the grass. By his side, Natalie fell to her knees and took his granddaughter into her arms as she ran up. The girl looked up at him and he saw the fear in her eyes.

'Grandfather,' she said. 'You did not come home last night.'

Moses gazed down at her.

All he had wanted was to take back the farm. To right the wrongs that had been done to his grandfather and to his father. His granddaughter looked up at him, her eyes wide with horror and around him across the neat stretch of lawn and the gravel drive, men roamed angry and bewildered. Moyo was laying still flat out on the grass. Roy had taken hold of the hose, while other men ran for pails of water. Kristine had her face buried in the pelt of her dog.

Moses reached out and took his granddaughter.

'This is our land,' he said to her. 'This is our farm.' But his voice was despondent.

'You think they will let you have this land?' Kristine said, her voice sharp and full of bitterness. 'Do you think it's on your behalf that they served those papers on us?'

Kristine stood up, and wiped her hands on the legs of her

jeans. There were dark marks smeared across her forehead and cheeks. Her face was set and hard.

'They've just been using you and the vets, Moses,' she said. 'Can't you see that? Mugabe will give this land to one of his supporters, one of the ZANU PF men from the area. Nobody is going to give you this farm, Moses. Nobody cares that it used to belong to your grandfather. The children are starving, a quarter of the population have AIDs. There are no schools. Is this a government that cares about its people?'

She walked across the grass to him. For a moment they stood facing each other in silence. Memories clung to her grandfather. Natalie stood close by, watching.

'We aren't the enemy any more, Moses,' Kristine said, her voice softer. 'The struggle against Ian Smith, against the old regime, that was legitimate. But now… ' She held her hands up in the air. 'We're not the enemy any longer.'

Christopher Moyo walked up and stood behind Moses. Natalie noticed Boyle eye them. He still carried his rifle, but it was slung now on his back as he coordinated the men bringing the pails of water to throw on the flames. Some of the veterans had joined the line of men, passing buckets from hand to hand. The flames had died down, though the smoke still rose thickly. The young man who had thrown the torch on the roof of the house was sat beneath the jacaranda tree, leant against the wide, old trunk, his head in his hands. One of Boyle's men stood over him, rifle in his hands.

'And what about us, Moses?' Kristine was saying. 'This is my home. Our daughter was born here. Where are we supposed to go?'

Moses looked at her, and though he looked suddenly shrunken and defeated, his gaze was still cold and defiant.

'You can go wherever you want,' he said. 'You are white. The world is open to you and your children.' He placed his hand on his granddaughter's head. 'Nobody will open their doors for us.'

Epilogue

31

Natalie saw the rain approaching as they came over the top of the hill. Memories walked a couple of paces in front of her. She nodded when Natalie pointed to the clouds and indicated with her left hand a great flame tree. They took shelter under the large hanging bough of the old tree. Memories stood close to her and she smelt the comfortable mousey smell of her. Memories looked up and smiled. Natalie smiled back sadly.

'I'm glad you came to see me,' Natalie said.

'Grandfather would not be happy,' she said with a grin. 'He does not want me talking with you. All the time he tells me the stories about the past, about his father and his grandfather.' She waved her hand as if swatting away a fly. 'What is the past? I just want an education.'

The rain moved up the hill battering the flowers on the jacarandas, beating the leaves from the baobab and the mimosas. Soon the foot of the valley was lost from sight, and the village was engulfed, the frail column of smoke rising from its fires flattened to the ground. Half of the family had moved out from the village since the occupation of the farm. Moses had claimed some land up close to the edge of the farm, beneath Drew's Kopje and close to the ridge where the caves were. It wasn't particularly profitable land and Roy had been happy to see him on it.

Moses wasn't the problem, Roy knew, he was just a pawn. The thatch on the roof of the house had been badly burned on one side, but they had covered it with tarpaulin and the inside of the house was undamaged. Most of the veterans had drifted away as the sun rose and around lunch time a police car drew up. Roy stood in the shade of the doorway with Kristine and Natalie and watched them. Boyle handed over the man who has started the fire and the police took him away.

Sunday was quiet. Roy walked around the farm with Bhekinkosi, assessing the damage that had been caused. Half of the workers had slipped away as the veterans invaded the farm.

'They're frightened, *bhasa*,' Bhekinkosi said, when Roy spoke to him. 'They don't want to get beaten.

Roy nodded. He knew they would wait and see what happened. As soon as they knew it was safe they would come back. He would get his solicitor to challenge the eviction papers on Monday morning. It would buy them some time.

When the rain had eased off, Natalie and Memories moved on across the ridge and down, following a narrow path, skirting the large granite boulders that balanced precariously along the hilltop. Memories led the way. She was dressed in her red T-shirt, with its white trimming, and beneath that the grey skirt, with its pocket hanging loose.

The path opened up suddenly into a little clearing. Dark, wet sand and coarse grass surrounded by trees and bushes. The heat was intense and the air heavy with the evaporating water, now the sun had come back out. Natalie opened the buttons of her blouse and flapped it in an attempt to cool down.

'Here,' Memories said.

'Why here?' Natalie asked, looking around the dreary patch of land.

'It's a sacred place,' Memories said. 'There are spirits here. The spirit of the hyena.'

'The hyena?'

Memories shook her head and grinned ruefully. 'I don't know, it's a story my grandfather tells.'

Memories walked across the clearing to a small mound around which had been placed stones. Though there were animal tracks, the grave had not been disturbed.

'They buried him deep, so that the animals would not dig him out,' Memories explained.

She squatted down beside the earth and Natalie knelt beside her. The grave was little more than a couple of feet square. Memories wiped the pebbles, which were covered in mud from the downfall of rain.

'This is where he's buried?' she said softly, almost to herself.

Memories nodded. 'This is where we buried him.'

Natalie pictured the tiny child. She felt the slight weight of him in her arms as she had lifted him from the rock. She recalled the way that he had moved, his eyes opening, looking up into hers. It was the first time she could recall picking up a baby. The first time that she had held a child. He was almost no weight at all. She had gazed down into his eyes and felt such a deep connection.

A hard bubble rose within her.

'Happiness,' she murmured.

And then she was crying. And she felt stupid before Memories but she couldn't stop herself. The tears flowed down her cheeks and dripped off onto the sandy grave and she felt a deep stabbing pain in her chest.

'Are you okay?'

Memories peered at her from the other side of the circle, but for some moments she could not answer. She pressed the heels of her hands into her eyes and took a deep, jagged breath of damp air. She had not cried. Not once during the whole process, during those horrible black weeks after the loss of her child had she cried.

'I'm sorry,' she said.

Memories gazed at her curiously.

'It's not about Happiness,' she explained. 'Well, kind of it is. I don't know how to express it.' She paused and looked up and wiped her face with the sleeve of her blouse. 'I was going to have a child,' she explained. 'Back in England. I was pregnant.'

Memories watched her. When Natalie didn't say anything more she asked, 'What happened?'

Natalie looked up at her. Her small delicate features, the soft curve of her face, her eyes, dark, wide, inquisitive.

'I lost it,' she said, and the tears came again. 'I had a miscarriage.' She paused, but Memories was watching her closely.

'A miscarriage,' she repeated, straightening up, wiping her face. 'Do you know what that is?'

Memories nodded.

Natalie paused, her mind reeling back across the months, to those moments when she rushed to the hospital. How it had been in the days afterwards. The sudden darkness. The unbearable sense of loss.

It had been late; she was into the third trimester and when she had first suspected something was wrong they had sent her back home from the hospital. Lawrence had tried to calm her, but when after a few days she had felt no movement she began to really worry. The midwife took out the handheld ultra sound and spread the gel across her belly. She had smiled and squeezed Natalie's hand. 'Don't worry,' she said.

How many seconds had it taken for panic to set in? She watched the midwife's face with fierce attention and saw immediately something was wrong.

Lawrence had come to pick her up from the hospital as soon as he had heard the news. He was caring and sad and had cried and for some reason she had hated him then. When he said he would stay the night with her, she did not let him.

'I'm fine,' she had said, not crying. 'Go home, you have work tomorrow.'

For some days she lay in her bed staring up at the ceiling. Lawrence called, but she did not answer the phone. She did not want to speak to him.

'I found it hard,' Natalie explained.

She glanced up at Memories, and then up, above her head to the kopje that rose up against the clearing sky. The hard rock jutted out, dark against the cerulean brightness of the heavens.

'That's why I came out here,' she said. 'I couldn't cope.' She paused, then continued. 'We were due to get married, the father of the child and I, but something inside me was broken. It affected us, the way that we were with each other.'

She waved her hand to indicate the things she could not say. Memories looked at her quietly, saying nothing.

'I never got to hold the child,' Natalie said. 'My baby.'

For some time they sat in silence. The air was heavy and pulsed with the steady rhythm of the cicadas. The clouds had gone now and the sky was perfectly clear, pale blue and the sun shone on them brightly.

'I'm sorry,' Memories said softly.

Natalie smiled sadly. 'Thank you,' she said.

'We found out who left the baby,' Memories said, a little later looking down at the grave.

Natalie wiped her face. 'Did you? Who?'

'She was from another village further north. The mother died soon after childbirth. There was nobody left to look after the baby, only an older brother. He was ten.'

'Your age?'

'I am twelve.'

'And the father?' Natalie asked.

'He had died. He had AIDs.'

Natalie looked across the small grave at Memories; her face was serious but the tone of her voice was matter-of-fact. Natalie shook her head. She took off a small silver cross that she wore around her neck. It was something Lawrence had bought for her at a craft market. She laid it on the grave. Slowly she got to her feet.

'So the boy took the baby up to the kopje?'

'He said that he did not know what to do with it.' Memories shrugged. She gazed at the small silver cross glittering in the dust where Natalie had laid it. 'It's not unusual,' Memories continued, 'many people die of AIDs or of other things. Many people do not have enough to eat.'

The girl stood up and brushed the dirt from her dress. Her eyes lingered still on the silver cross.

'Would you like it?' Natalie asked.

Memories' eyebrows rose quizzically.

'The cross,' Natalie clarified. She bent down and picked it up. 'It's a shame to leave it here.'

'Somebody would find it and take it,' Memories agreed.

Natalie stepped closer to the girl and slipped the chain over her head. The cross shone brightly against her dark skin.

'Thank you,' Memories said.

'It's so very little,' Natalie said. 'So very little.'

So, no myths, she thought. No hyenas, no tales – just poverty and disease on a scale that I cannot even begin to comprehend.

Later they walked back up the path, to the ridge that overlooked the farm. For a moment they paused and looked down the long green slope to the valley spread out below and, at the foot of the hill, the farm and the pale thread of road that wriggled down to Bindura.

'I'm sorry about the school,' Natalie said. 'I've let you down.'

Memories leant against her and grinned, linking her arm through Natalie's. 'Thank you for the lessons, teacher,' she said.

'What will you do?' Natalie asked as they worked their way down the steep path, walking slowly, taking care as the ground was still wet in the shade and slippery.

'There is a school in Bindura,' she said. '*Sekuru* – grandfather – said that I could go. He said that he would arrange it. His father was good at school; he went to university in South Africa and became a teacher. *Sekuru* says that I must be like his father, because I like studying.'

Natalie smiled.

Memories stepped forward, skipping lightly across a stream. 'I will be a teacher like you.' She grinned. 'And then I will come back here and teach. Will you go back to England to teach?'

Natalie glanced at her then gazed back down across the valley. The trees shimmered in the heat and the distant hills seemed to recede. The valley was verdantly green after the weeks of rain. She felt a sudden deep, intense love for this landscape.

She thought about going back to England. She thought about Lawrence and what they had. She could go back to him and rebuild what had been lost, mend some of the damage that had been done and try again. Perhaps think about having another child.

'No,' she said, turning to Memories. When she spoke again the words came out more passionately than she had intended. 'You can't go back. You cannot relive what was. You can mourn it, you can regret its passing, but you shouldn't try to recreate something that has gone.' She paused. 'I'm going to Botswana for a couple of months,' she said to Memories. 'And then possibly down to South Africa to see Barbara. After that… '

She shrugged.

At the edge of the farm she said goodbye to Memories. Impulsively she bent forward and embraced the girl. Memories giggled and clung to her tightly.

'I'll miss you, teacher,' Memories said.

Natalie nodded. 'I'll miss you.' She touched the cross on the girl's chest. 'Take care.'

Memories walked north around the edge of the property. For some minutes Natalie stood in the shade of the jacaranda tree and watched her as she went. She turned once and smiled and waved and Natalie waved back. Natalie watched her until she dissolved in the heat haze and only then did she turn back to the farmhouse.

Walking through the gates she recalled that morning when she had rode back beneath the tree and through the gates with the baby cradled in her arms.

In the cottage she sat down at her desk and picked up the photograph and for some moments gazed at it. In the photo she stood next to Lawrence. He had his arm around her shoulders and had a large grin on his face. She was smiling too, but her smile was more reserved, secretive. Her arm cradled her belly. She remembered the day distinctly.

She stroked the photograph gently with the tip of her finger. For a moment she felt lost.

She recalled the small grave of the little boy. She thought about the grave back in Lewisham, the tiny little plot beneath the extended shade of a beech tree that overhung the wall of the cemetery.

She sighed and tucked the photograph inside her diary, placing it in her bag.

32

Moses was tired after the walk up to the cave at the top of the kopje. He had forgotten what a climb it was. He wished Memories had been there with him to share the moment, but she had disappeared some hours before. For some moments he stood in the mouth of the cave and looked out over the land. Heat waves were rising from the trees and the sound of insects filled the air. There was no other sound; no cars, no machinery, no planes, it was as though the earth had been born anew and was back as it had been when his ancestors had farmed this land. He breathed in deeply, filling his lungs with the pure air.

He took a small pack from his back and opened it on the floor of the cave. Inside were a couple of cans of Eagle beer and a bowl of *sadza*. It would have been better to brew the beer himself, seven day beer, but he had not had time to do that. He spread the libations in front of him, cracked open one of beer cans and poured it over the floor of the cave.

'*Mudzimu*!' He called. 'Spirits, hear my call. I welcome you back home. Chimukoko, come to guide your family. Have patience with us. Treat us with mercy.'

His words echoed dully from the walls of the cave. In the silence after, he listened, his entire senses alert.

'*Mudzimu*!' he called again, louder now. 'Spirits!

Chimukoko!'

There was a sudden breath of air, a hot breeze that lifted the dust from the earth. Moses shuddered. He bowed his head to the floor of the cave.

'*Mudzimu*!' he whispered.

He heard the wind stir in the trees behind him. He heard the rumble of the thunder and the day was suddenly darkened. He heard the rustle of water on the leaves and its hiss on the dry earth behind him and he felt the presence of the spirits and his heart was filled with fear and joy. He pressed his forehead to the earth with the sound of the rain and the rumble of the thunder in his ears.

'Chimukoko, Tafawa, and Zindonga, my father,' he whispered. 'Your names will never be forgotten. One day this land will be ours again and you will be free to wander the pastures and to rest beneath the shade of the trees and to drink from the streams and to hunt the *duiker* in the fields and hills.'

We hope you enjoyed Stephan's novel. If you would like to read more, here are the first two chapters of *The Song of the Stork*. A beautifully atmospheric read, this tells the story of Yael, a young Jewish girl on the run. A story of love, hope and survival, this is one woman's story as she struggles to find her voice, while voices around her are extinguished.

1

They left the barn as soon as it was dark. Rivka had stood by the door watching as the light faded, moving from one foot to the other, anxious. When, finally, the shadows were deep enough, they slipped out, ears straining for sounds, stepping bare foot on the gravel, fear numbing the pain of the sharp stones that bit into the soft flesh of the soles of their feet.

The turned earth of the harvested fields was cool and soft after the gravel, but it was heavy going and they were tired before they had crossed halfway towards the forest that lipped the hilltop. Rivka coughed continuously into her sleeve, fearing the sound would travel back across the field.

They sank down when they reached the forest's edge. The moon had just risen and the field shone, illuminated. Rivka's face looked drawn.

"You're bleeding," Yael whispered, and reaching out wiped the streak of dark blood from her lips with the cuff of her sleeve.

"I must have bitten my lip," Rivka said.

"But look at your jacket," Yael pointed at the dark stain in the crook of her arm, into which Rivka had been coughing.

"Come on, we must move."

Rivka hauled herself up and turned towards the darkness of the woods.

"We must move as fast as we can."

Yael followed behind Rivka, arms in front, shielding her face against the supple pine branches that snapped back ferociously as Rivka pushed through them.

They covered no more than a couple of miles that night. Exhausted, they found a deep patch of undergrowth and wriggled into the centre of it, the brambles scratching at their faces, bloodying the backs of their hands and calves. Rivka fell asleep almost immediately. For some time, Yael watched her. Her body was emaciated, her cheeks sunken, the skin around her eyes loose and dark. Dried blood flecked her pale lips. Her hands looked like the hands of an old woman. Her breathing was fast, feverish. Her chest rose in a shallow, rapid rhythm. Yael sank down beside her, pulling her close. Covered their bodies with twigs and bracken. Rivka seemed to have shrunk. She was no longer the larger-than-life young woman Yael had first seen on the stage of the House of Culture in Selo, part of the young Yiddish theatre group.

Or perhaps, Yael thought, I've grown. She lifted her head and surveyed her own body. She too had grown thinner, but her body did not bear the same marks of sickness Rivka's did.

Her skin, she noted, was healthy-looking still, tight against her flesh. Her hair was thick, in fact uncomfortably so. She was tempted to take Rivka's knife and chop it off. It lay matted and itchy against the back of her neck.

Her skin was broken by an endless pattern of dried scabs where she had scratched at bites. She had begun to get used to the continual torment of the lice. Rivka had taken a cigarette lighter one day and forced Yael to undress. She had run the flame slowly up each seam. The lice crackled as they fried.

The night was cold and by morning a thick mist had gathered close to the earth. Yael shivered through the dark hours, her body pulled close against Rivka's, which seemed hot. She was, Yael realised, running a temperature. As the light began to seep through the brambles, Rivka began to shake. Her forehead was burning and her clothes were damp, not only with the cold mist, but with sweat.

"Rivka," Yael whispered into her ear.

The older woman muttered and turned, but did not open her eyes.

"We need to go back to the farm," Yael said.

But Rivka did not respond. Yael tried to lift her, but was unable to do so. Pushing out of the brambles she wandered around for a while and finally found a small stream. She cupped her hands and drank some water and then looked around for something to carry water back for Rivka, but there was nothing.

In the end she took off her blouse, from beneath the man's jacket. She coiled the blouse and dipped it in the water until it was soaked. She carried it back and twisted it gently above Rivka's lips. The water ran from her lips down her face, dirty. She held a corner of the cold wet cloth against Rivka's fevered forehead.

For the rest of the day she sat like that, moving occasionally to bathe the blouse in the stream. There were berries in the brambles and she picked and ate them. She tried to get Rivka to eat, but she was unwilling.

As night fell, Rivka seemed to improve. She opened her eyes and half sat up, leaning against Yael.

"I'm sorry," she muttered. "I'm so sorry."

"Don't be silly," Yael said, stroking her skin with the damp cool cloth of her blouse. "You'll be better soon."

"Yes." Rivka smiled weakly and tried to pull herself up higher. She ate some berries Yael crushed between her lips and drank some water from the twisted wet blouse on her tongue.

When Yael woke the next morning, Rivka felt cooler by her side. She reached across and touched the skin of her forehead with the back of her fingers. The temperature had definitely gone. She sat up.

"Rivka," she whispered, and shook her softly.

Her body was stiff.

"Rivka?" Yael called, her throat constricting.

Rivka's eyes were closed. When Yael turned her over, she found blood congealed at the corner of her mouth and in the rim of her nostrils. She looked astonishingly calm and it struck Yael, as she gazed at her in disbelief, that it had been a long time since she had seen her face look so calm.

For the rest of morning she sat silently beside Rivka's body, holding her cold hand. A hard lump pressed at her throat but she did not cry.

Later she covered the body with a thick layer of leaves and fronds of fern that were dark green and succulent. She laid them deeply, until there was no hint a body was there. Then she crawled out from the brambles and turned back towards Czeslaw's farm.

2

Standing at the edge of the fields, shaded by the thick branches of the fir trees, Yael stood gazing down on the farm. The yard was thick with German military vehicles and soldiers milled around the barn and the house. Camouflaged tents were erected around the edge of the field. She heard shouts and the sound of laughter. The farmer mingled with the soldiers, passing around bottles. Smoke from a fire rose steadily into the cool still air. She and Rivka had left just in time.

Yael turned and pushed back through the branches into the wood. She wandered aimlessly. She had no idea where she might turn. For some time she sat on the rotting trunk of a fallen tree, head in hands. She considered going back to the shtetl, but knew that would be madness. From her pocket she took Rivka's handgun. She ran her fingers along the cold metal barrel, turned it and placed the muzzle of it against the soft skin between her eyes. She could just rest her finger now against the thin trigger and that would be it, she thought. She felt an icy shiver across her skin. She put it away quickly.

Getting up, she wandered away from the farm.

"Oh Josef," she muttered to herself, thinking of her brother who she had not seen in a year now. "Where are you?"

From the position of the pale risen sun, she orientated herself and began to make her way northeast in the direction of the Russian front. She had little idea how far the Germans had managed to press the Soviets back. Perhaps they had already won the war, she thought. Perhaps the Russians had admitted defeat.

But she pictured Josef in Red Army uniform on the back of his horse. Never, she thought. He would never admit defeat. There would be more like him.

A couple of miles north, the forest ended suddenly. A dirt road wound down into a low valley. In the centre of the small valley stood a dilapidated farmhouse, with tumbling outbuildings leaned against it. She recognised where she was, though she had only seen the farm once, from the back of a cart that had brought her from the train station in Grodno.

The farm belonged to Aleksei, the idiot. 'He's not crazy,' she remembered her father saying as they bumped along the road, after their trip to Warsaw.

'He just doesn't like company.'

'He doesn't speak,' her mother had said, as if that fact alone was enough to prove his madness.

'And that makes him a *meshúgener*?' her father had retorted. 'Then give me more of them! Give me a whole *shtetl* of *meshúgener*! I could live in such a place.'

Every village had somebody that was crazy. The odd ones. In Selo they had Able. Able had the mind of a child, though his beard was long and his hair beginning to grey. He was a simple and pleasant man who begged for sweets outside the shop and cried when the boys from the town made fun of him. One of Yael's sweetest memories of her brother was the time he had chased off Marek Wolniewicz and his friends who had been tormenting Able. He had gone to the shop and bought some boiled sweets which Able had received with pitiful joy. The thought of it now stabbed her heart with a small pain of longing for the company of her brother.

And then there was Aleksei. His father died when he was a teenager. The story in the village was that he had never spoken, that he had some medical problem that rendered him mute, but there were some who thought differently.

'He spoke as child,' Myra Koppelman asserted. 'I remember visiting his poor mother when he was a toddler and he talked all right then. It was her dying in the way she did that stopped his mouth.'

'That's rubbish,' her husband Eli Koppelman argued. 'He never spoke a word in his life. He isn't able. He has a problem. Doctor Sonenson told me.'

'Sonenson? What does he know?'

Everybody had assumed that when his father died some relative would come and take the teenager, or that he would be sent to live in one of the hostels, but he had refused to move from the farm. He carried on working there, eking out a subsistence from his fields, occasionally trading vegetables or a pig for some goods he could not produce himself. He kept to himself and rarely came to the village, preferring to deal with the couple of nearby farmers he trusted.

She settled down in the woods, not far from the farm and waited for darkness.

For Marija

Acknowledgements

My thanks to Annette Green and Lauren Parsons for the acuity of their editorial suggestions and their general warm support. I would also like to thank the many friends in Zimbabwe who offered their friendship and opened their homes, noting, particularly Clara and Yvonne for the laughter and for teaching me to sing Shona songs.